Sheenah Middle

Jack

First published by Sheenah Middle in 2017

Copyright © Sheenah Middle, 2017

All rights reserved. No part of this publication may be reproduced, stored, or transmitted in any form or by any means, electronic, mechanical, photocopying, recording, scanning, or otherwise without written permission from the publisher. It is illegal to copy this book, post it to a website, or distribute it by any other means without permission.

This book was professionally typeset on Reedsy.
Find out more at reedsy.com

Contents

Prologue	i
Chapter 1	1
Chapter 2	9
Chapter 3	15
Chapter 4	21
Chapter 5	27
Chapter 6	32
Chapter 7	37
Chapter 8	43
Chapter 9	49
Chapter 10	54
Chapter 11	58
Chapter 12	63
Chapter 13	69
Chapter 14	75
Chapter 15	81
Chapter 16	86
Chapter 17	93
Chapter 18	98
Chapter 19	105
Chapter 20	109
Chapter 21	113
Chapter 22	118

Chapter 23	124
Chapter 24	130
Chapter 25	134
Chapter 26	138
Chapter 27	141
Chapter 28	145
Chapter 29	148
BIBLIOGRAPHY	153

Prologue

If you are wondering why I wrote this story. Well, as a child and young teenager I had a fascination for old black and white films and Hammer Horror. I would sit up on a Saturday night after my friends had gone home and waiting for my Dad to come home with a Chinese, watching all the old films on the BBC.

Dad would come back, sometimes with friends and sometimes it was just the two of us staying up to the early hour watching Frankenstein, Dr Jekyll and Mr Hyde, or Dracula, eating the food.

As we all know the stories were based on classics or actual events and it gave me a thirst for wanting to know more. I was not happy just reading classics; I wanted to read the books that inspired the films.

There are a lot of them out there ...

With my imagination piqued, so many years ago, I decided to write a story about someone from those films. And 5 years ago I started.

With the web at hand, I started investigating some of the characters from the movies and slowly Jack, was born.

He didn't start out as Jack, that took time. My first thought was to find out who the man, or woman was and what drove them. But I didn't want to just write another Ripper story, I wanted something that grew from the myth.

That led to me setting the story today, but again I didn't want a spin off, I wanted a way of telling the story of Jack in 1888, but in the current environment.

My first thoughts were to try to solve it. (I can't do worse than the other theories out there!) But while I was researching, I came across this ...

Whodunit? : Choosing a Ripper Suspect
Andrew L Morrison

Since 1888 those that have been named as possibly being Jack the Ripper must number in their hundreds and that's just the ones we know about! How do you decide on a suspect? The answer to that depend on the criteria that you choose.

Does there have to be incontrovertible proof that the suspect really existed? If the answer is yes then Dr Stanley is not an option as it has never been conclusively proved that he did exist. "I plead not guilty of the crimes of which I am accused your honour on the grounds that I am a fictional creation." does appear a rather good defence! Until recently Michael Ostrog was also in this category but research in recent years has proven his existence.

Does the suspect have to have an East End connection? If so then Joseph Barnett and Donston are possibilities. How much of a connection is needed? Does having chambers at King's Bench Walk and a mother in an asylum at Clapton (Druitt) count or visiting at intervals from Liverpool (Maybrick)?

Is proof that the suspect knew at least one of the victims necessary? Again Joseph Barnett fits the bill as does George Hutchinson and Michael Kidney but so too does Dr Barnardo who claimed to have met Liz Stride only days before her murder and he spent a lot of time in the East End!

How many victims were there? If it's more than five and Alice McKenzie and Francis Coles are included then Druitt is ruled out as he died in December 1888 as is Tumblety who fled the country. The

Maybrick diary only mentions the five usual victims so if there were more, or indeed less, he is also removed from the frame.

What about the various supposed Ripper writings? If the dear boss letter is genuine does it point towards an American? If the letter sent along with a kidney to George Lusk was really from the killer then it suggests a certain amount of theatricality and could have come from a poet (J K Stephen) or a bad actor (Druitt, whose Sir Toby Belch at school was better imagined than described).The Goulston Street graffito if written by the Ripper could point towards somebody who carried chalk in their pockets like a schoolteacher (Druitt). If the message is supposed to accuse the Jews then does that mean the killer was not a Jew or that he was and wanted to get other Jews into trouble? In this case the spelling "Juwes" suggests an uneducated person and not a schoolteacher, Cambridge scholar etc. Is Juwes a masonic term and if so does this mean a masonic conspiracy?

Did the killer show any medical skills? If so then Donston, Tumblety, Gull, Cream are some obvious choices. Would Druitt, who was not a doctor but came from a family of doctors, have enough skill? Could a butcher or Shochet have done it or was there no skill involved at all?

Should the suspects be limited to those named in police sources, official or otherwise? This would make the main candidates Druitt, Ostrog, Kosminski (named by Macnaghten), Tumblety (named by Littlechild), Chapman (named by Abberline) Donston (name in police files) plus a number of people like Barnett, Hutchinson and Kidney who were mentioned in relation to the case. Did the police know who the killer was? If they did and did not reveal the culprit then that suggests a conspiracy which in turn suggests the killer was important. Freemasons perhaps or a prince of the realm?

Should known murderers head the suspects list such as Chapman, Cream, Deeming, James Kelly and or should they be dismissed because their modus operandi was different from the Ripper's?

The above shows some of the many questions that must be answered before a suspect can be settled on. Even when one is chosen that is not the end of the difficulties. The theory must be made to fit the facts and not the other way round. "Facts" which strengthen the case of a suspect should not be blindly accepted and those that weaken the case should not be blindly ignored. The one certainty in the mystery of Jack the Ripper is that one can never be absolutely certain who was guilty. As Donald Rumbelow wrote "...the answer must always be 'Perhaps'. It can only remain conjecture."

I read this one night before going to bed, the next morning the whole story changed, I was no longer going to solve, I was going to tell a story and …

Well, now it is up to you to read it and decide if I did the story justice.

One last thing, you may need to find a good Scottish translator! This is the one I used to help me.

http://www.scotranslate.com

I hope you enjoy it.

Sheenah xx

1

Ed woke up that morning in a dark, melancholic mood that had gripped him so many mornings before. He reached for his notepad and started writing down the dream he had just experienced.

On mornings like today, these dreams or visions were more like nightmares, with all the realism he found in them. Ed would wake from them with the sharp smell of the streets and the people still in his nostrils. He, like most people, was aware of the horrific events of the late 19th century. But these visions were worse than the stories told in books and on film. He was in a killer's mind. That was the only thing that he could think of to explain what was going on. This mind he was in was psychotic, and he was scared that it would eventually possess him entirely.

Maybe he should see his doctor, again? But he didn't relish being told he was suffering from something like depression or bipolar disorder or maybe something worse. Yes, he advised that there was nothing wrong, that the dreams were just that. But they were getting more intense, and he was feeling more of the other person's hatred of women.

Every morning when he woke up like this, he would always question the reason why this was happening to him. From the third one, when he had experienced the attack on that poor woman called Emma, to the one last night. He always thought there was so much that was going unanswered, and he hoped it would soon end.

He got out of bed, shaking the last residue of his sleep from his head, and grabbed a towel off the radiator before stepping out into the hall and then the bathroom, in the next room. Sitting on the toilet, he reflected on how his life had changed in the short few months since these visions had started. Ed had felt many emotions watching the story unfold night after night; he just wished he could get it all down on paper, that somehow he could convey the story to other people. He just couldn't express the horror it left within him.

He reached over and started the shower, and after flushing the toilet, he stepped under the hot and steamy water.

While he was rinsing the shower gel from his body, he again went back to the question of what he was still doing in Glasgow. Maybe if he went back home, then life would return to normality. Well, perhaps to a more conscious existence than it was at the moment. But this was a great place to live. It was cheaper than Surrey, and the nightlife was great.

He knew that sooner or later he would have to get out and work; the money he had inherited from his uncle wouldn't last forever. But he wanted to be a writer, and living this far away from his mother had helped him grow and develop that idea. Yet if he wanted to keep away from her and her plans to entrench him in the family business, Ed would have to finish this novel quickly and prove to her that he could do it. On his own.

His mother had always been quick to point out that he was going to need another source of income. To find another way to support the variety of "nasty habits" he had seemed to have picked up while "going around with the wrong crowd", as

CHAPTER 1

she stated on many occasions. However, they both knew that wasn't the only reason he was staying away from the family home. He had needed to move away from her domineering manner. Maybe his father was happy to be henpecked and bullied by her, but he wasn't and, yes, he loved her – as any son should their mother – but he needed to make it on his own. He also knew that she needed to let him go and allow him to make his mistakes on his own.

He hauled himself out of the shower and looked in the large square mirror over the sink; using the flannel to wipe away the condensation, he started to brush his teeth. God, he looked ill. His eyes had a haunted gaze about them, and he had noticed the black rings under them. The dreams were making him restless but, until this story had come to a conclusion, he knew that this would not change. He was glad today he didn't have that nagging headache.

His hair had that tousled look from the towel drying he had given it, so he ran his fingers through it and tidied it down. He finished towelling himself down and returned the damp towel to the radiator. He pulled on a shirt and pair of jeans that were hanging on a chair by the bed, only after giving them a quick sniff. Yes, they would do one more day.

He was living on the top floor in an impressive traditional two-bedroom flat within an attractive red sandstone tenement building in the heart of Hyndland that dated back to the beginning of the 20th century. With entire areas in Glasgow succumbing to demolishment and being readied for renovation, he felt lucky to have bought this property and even more fortunate that it now had a preservation order on it.

Ed had researched the history of the building when he had first found the two-bedroom property. It had intrigued him to know the history of these homes. Glasgow in 1850 until around 1914 was awash with these grey, beige and red sandstone tenements. The four-storeyed blocks were not allowed to be taller than the width of the street. Each of the properties benefitted from a small garden; there were also clothes drying areas and an outside lavatory or ash pits at the centre of the block.

With Scotland's growth in heavy industries during the 19th century, there was a huge migration of workers from the Highlands and Ireland. The tenements, as the buildings that would come to house them were known, were seen as an improvement to the overcrowding these employees and their families initially found themselves in when they first got to the cities. They were also a better way of getting more people into smaller areas. However, as Ed had discovered, the tenements became an overcrowded and unsanitary place to live, with the growing immigration and slowly developing into slums.

So here he was living in one of those flats. Now seen as a safe area, that was spacious enough for him with some great neighbours.

Thinking back to his dreams and the conditions of the streets he visited while asleep, it had opened up his mind to the perils of life in Victorian Britain. Maybe if this Jack the Ripper book sold well, he could look at the lives of the residents in the Gorbals or the like to see if there was a story there.

His mother had despaired of him when he had said he was going to study English Literature at Edinburgh. As a child, he had always had the most vivid dreams and had enjoyed putting them to paper or narrating them to a captive audience on Christmas Day.

It had been his uncle that had understood and encouraged

CHAPTER 1

him, while his parents had wanted him to inherit the family printing firm, like his grandfather and great-grandfather before him. But now it was just him against them, with no uncle to battle his case for him.

Uncle Frank had been an actor and the black sheep of his mother's family, but he had been successful. He may not have been an A-list Hollywood star, though he had made a few good British-backed films in the 1950s and '60s, with a few good leads and a lot of cameo parts. It was in the latter part of his life that Frank had acquired a semi-major role in a famous soap opera. All of which had paid him well and, to his sister's amazement, Frank had invested well.

When he had suffered his fatal heart attack two years ago, the family had been shocked and dismayed to discover that Frank had left the entire fortune to Ed, the whole three million pounds. This unexpected windfall had bought Ed this flat and furnished it. Like his uncle, Ed too had invested the rest and was living off the interest. But interest rates, as they were, meant that he found that he was starting to live off some of the capital.

Ed moved into the kitchen and put the kettle on while opening the packet of Regal cigarettes he had perched on the side. Ed placed one of the smokes in his mouth. He used an orange lighter to light it and inhaled that first nicotine fix of the day. Ed, at the very tender age of 24, had started smoking in school and had "never intended to quit". This first fix of the day was all he needed to prove that Ed would miss it if he stopped. It was something Ed could not give up: that and coffee. Yes, he had heard the arguments and read the literature and heard the stories of ex-smokers who had said the desire to smoke passed over time, but he lived for that feeling.

Outside, the noises of the hustle and bustle of the city waking up drew him over to the window that looked down on the side street. As he peered down at the people milling around, he sipped the high caffeine coffee – black, of course; he had forgotten to get milk the day before. It looked like it could snow today. That is one thing he would miss if he moved back home, the snow. He loved it, that and the diversity of the seasons in Scotland.

He wondered what he should do today. It was the first Tuesday in December, and with Christmas just weeks away, Ed thought that maybe he should shop. He wasn't going to be able to go home to London without being weighed down with presents for everybody. His mother had told him that if he wanted to live away from the fold like the prodigal son, then while visiting, he should show his thanks for the privilege.

He finished his drink, placing the cup in the sink and, after putting on his big black wool coat, he ventured out into the morning. He walked to the bus stop and waited for the bus to the city centre while smoking yet another cigarette. A few people were waiting there, and he smiled at an old lady as she joined the queue. She scowled back at him; the older generation didn't trust his generation.

Glasgow city centre is an eclectic mixture of Victorian and modern design. It has a distinct architecture, with elements of 19th-century Victorian architecture alongside early 20th-century 'Glasgow Style', developed by Charles Rennie Mackintosh. In recent years, new shopping malls could be seen opening up, giving residents and visitors a warm reprieve from the harsh wind that blew down the streets. After spending more than an hour in John Lewis and buying nothing, he decided he needed that caffeine fix again, so he made his way to his

CHAPTER 1

favourite coffee shop on Royal Exchange Square.

He had spent many mornings in this little café with either a hangover or sometimes on his way home from some girl's place that he had woken up in; that had been in the first eighteen months he had lived here. Now there was just one young lady in his life: Sandi, who happened to live in one of the flats just around the corner to where he sat now.

They had been seeing each other for about six months, and he had wanted her to move in with him, but she was unsure. Her argument had been that she didn't wish to be with someone who seemed to be doing nothing. Yes, she understood about him taking time out, but she felt Ed should join the real world and that his mother did have a point. Now with them both going down to visit his parents over the Christmas break, he hoped she would understand his reasons for drifting, that she would realise his resentment of the destiny set out before him.

She lived in a two-bedroom flat that she shared with her oldest friend, Lesley. It was close to where she worked, and it was cheap. Her chosen job involved working with disadvantaged children. It was part of her character that having graduated from university with an English degree, she should end up doing social work. She was always trying to improve society and was very active in little projects that seemed to come her way. It was one of the things that had drawn him to her. He didn't understand her devotion to the underprivileged, but he admired her for it.

And he did love her as she did him.

He knew she would be in her flat getting ready for work. She was working a late shift. He imagined her as she combed her hair, brushing her teeth and searching through her wardrobe for something to wear. She was very fussy about making the correct impression on people, unlike him, who was content just to make do with whatever he could find that was reasonably clean and comfortable.

He was tempted to walk over to her flat and then thought better of it. She would be irritated because it was interrupting her before her shift began. She was a very private person and needed boundaries. It would have to wait until tonight. Instead, he carried on with his people watching, as he sipped the latté in front of him.

He was sat outside smoking and sipping his coffee, pondering what to do with himself for the rest of the day, when he saw Sandi stroll across the square towards her place of work. He sent her a text complimenting her on the choice of boots. She had texted back telling him to get back to his writing and that she would see him that night, with a winking emoji.

He turned away and looked back up the street relishing how this city had changed, how it seemed so much more of a vibrant place, not the worn out place he had been led to believe it was. He had grown to love this town and its inhabitants.

2

"Weel, morn tae ye maister, ah main say ye ur lookin' huir uv a braw the-day," came a deep, growling voice in a broad Scottish accent behind him. Like every major city in the world, homeless people were living on the street of Glasgow. They blocked the doorways and slept on park benches, while the much privileged seemed blinkered to their suffering. It didn't help that the media had shown the wrong side of the homeless, the ones who had taken it up as a profession to beg for money and were seeming to make a good living at it.

But that was only a small minority of these people. The real homeless didn't beg. They didn't hound you for that £1 coin for a 'cuppa'. They went about their business not bothering anyone. They learnt where to get the out-of-date food, what bins Tesco used and when. They knew when the off-licence discarded the old beer. That is how they survived, that and the helping hand of the Salvation Army and other charities set up to help them.

As the man behind Ed had placed a hand on his shoulder, he realised just how happy he was to hear that voice. Ed knew that this cold weather could take the homeless quickly, and not for the first time he wondered who would be there to grieve for Weegie or any of these people.

Ed laughed; he had had many a conversation with Weegie

over the past two years, although he still had problems understanding the accent. On the few times the two had met Sandi together, she had been their translator, and even she had admitted to sometimes having problems understanding him.

"Weegie," Ed said greeting him, offering him one of the empty seats at the table. It was not his given name, but it was the name he had been known by for many years. Most people didn't know his real name or who he was in his previous life, or why he was living on the streets, but he was well known within the community and surprisingly well liked.

"Would you like coffee?" asked Ed as he leant back a bit in his chair, knowing this was now going to be an enjoyable hour or so. He picked up the packet of cigarettes and offered one to Weegie while exhaling a curl of smoke from the one he had lit in his hand.

He was one of the most charismatic people Ed had met in his short time in this city. Weegie was well known for helping out anyone where he could. Many had seen him carry an old ladies' 'messages' or, as Ed would call them, shopping home. 'Messages' always struck Ed as such a quaint Scottish word.

Weegie had also been seen, many times, helping a struggling mother with a pushchair up a flight of stairs. Because he would never take money as a tip, his remuneration was always a pouch of tobacco or a bottle of beer.

Weegie smiled. Ed felt that with that white beard and shabby coat pulled together with a wide black belt he looked like Father Christmas. The belt was straining to hold another coat and two jackets tight against his body. It was enough to keep the wind out, and Weegie did look warm. The thing that surprised Ed was that today Weegie smelled of soap and washing powder. That was a bit of a surprise because, on most days when he encountered him, there was normally a wood-and-ash smell about him. Weegie never had a nasty smell about him; it was more like a bonfire. Ed guessed he was taking advantage of the annual shelters that opened up for the homeless, giving them a hot, well tepid, shower, an evening meal and, if they were lucky, a sleeping bag on the floor.

"Och, Mr Ryder, 'at woods be guid. Ah, hink thaur coods be snaw by dusk." Ed called the waiter over, who was not too happy to see this dirty, smelly-looking homeless man take a seat, but he knew the other man could and would pay.

Money was money, no matter who paid the bill. At least they were outside, the waiter contemplated as he moved over to take the order, and the afternoon was quiet so there shouldn't be too many complaints. The promised snow was keeping people away. He would have preferred being home and playing that new game he picked up yesterday. Working in the winter was such a drag. Work was a drag full stop.

"Haw is th' book comin' oan? Hae ye finished it?" Weegie asked.

"No. I haven't started it yet. I think I am having problems with the subject and whether people want to read another Jack the Ripper story. I think I am scared it will be crap. The subject is so old school and has been hashed about so often before. Would a new take on it work? Would it sell?" He turned his head to the waiter, "Two coffees, please, and just bring out some of those sandwiches, too." Ed gestured to the counter inside. "Any will do."

"Yoo ken, Mr Ryder, it reminds me when Ah lived in Paisley as a bairn, back in sixty yin, or twa an' Ah went it skitin' wi' Tam Conti. He was tellin' me abit his dreams. Tam hud juist stairted his acting joab an' was scared, but look at heem noo?

An' Ah bit he still remembers me."

Ed listened intently, trying to figure out who this man was exactly. From the conversations that the two of them had had over the years, Ed had learnt that Weegie had come from a very wealthy family. His parents had been landowners, and Weegie had inherited a large estate, but that wasn't how Weegie wanted to be, as he had tried to tell Ed. It hadn't made him happy inside. Weegie had talked many times of the emptiness he had felt, and even his marriage hadn't helped.

He had married Fiona, a very attractive woman, shortly after they met back in 1974. He was 24, two years her senior. By 1983, they had four children, three girls and one boy, and lived in a substantial house with land on Sandy Road, Seamill, West Kilbride.

In the mid-1980s, he had everything he could have ever wanted: expensive cars, a boat and staff, as well as the perfect family. However, Weegie had a problem. Despite all his wealth, Weegie's depression had worsened. He felt very empty and alone, as well as suicidal.

The worst was he had kept it hidden away from his wife and family. Weegie had told Ed about his lack of courage to tell his wife that he struggled every morning to get out of bed, to actually function. He hated socialising and it was quite common for Fiona to throw a dinner or drinks party and Weegie would fail to utter a word the whole night. It became a bit of a joke as well as a challenge for people to try to get him to speak. When this got too much, Weegie started making excuses to leave.

In those days, unlike today, mental health wasn't discussed. It was taboo. You just shrugged it off and got on with it. You were just 'under the weather'. The problem that worried Weegie more was that he believed that if you were really deeply depressed, you were taken away and treated in asylums, away from society. He had read and heard that the treatment could be barbaric and not always successful. Anti-depressants were in their infancy and not as readily available as they are today.

The other stigma that struck Weegie was that within the middle and upper classes, depression was seen as a sign of weakness; it was not something that happened to people with money, to people who had everything. What did they have to be sad about? Within Weegie's own circle of friends, there was not one person he could turn to. Even going to visit his doctor wasn't something he considered. He felt that nobody would understand and he would lose everything.

And his biggest fear was losing his wife's love.

The longer this went on, the unhappier Weegie became. He just wanted to be happy. But one day he decided to leave all the riches and unhappiness behind him. His fear of losing his family was so great that he believed he needed to let them go before they let him go. So much so that one day in May in the mid-1980s, he couldn't remember the exact date, but knew it was a Wednesday, he left. He took a change of clothes and some blankets, then getting on a train in the early hours of the morning, moved onto the streets of Glasgow.

It was a year later that he ran into a problem. He caught pneumonia and was taken to a local hospital. He was hanging on to life for a month, and it was touch and go whether he would make it. A nurse had gone through his pockets, hoping to find something that would help locate someone to inform them about his condition and found a photo of his family. The police were called in, and after a few inquiries, Fiona was found. She came alone to the hospital. She stayed for a brief visit, standing at the end of his bed, looking at him as he stared back, hoping she didn't hate him. It was a short time later that Fiona told the staff that she didn't know this man and that he was not the man who had gone missing the year before. Although the nurse who had stood in the room with Fiona and Weegie had wondered why the two of them had tears in their eyes as she left.

From this, it was concluded that he must have stolen the photo and coat from the real missing man and that the police would make further enquiries as to his whereabouts. When Weegie did recover shortly after this and was discharged, he was asked about the photo. Weegie told them that he must have found the coat behind some bins off Argyle Street. The police never made any headway in the search.

The hospital staff tried to get him to a homeless charity to get him off the streets, but he lasted one night before going back to his friends in the city centre.

Suddenly, Weegie's raspy, crackling laugh brought Ed back to reality, and Ed couldn't help but smile. He watched Weegie pull a half pouch of Golden Virginia out of his coat pocket and roll a thin cigarette with his gnarled old hand. "Do ye want?" Ed nodded and took it from his hand.

3

The conversation drifted into an afternoon of meaningless topics, while they ate, drank and smoked into the early evening and the first flurries of snow began to fall, from a darkening sky.

When he returned home shortly after nightfall, there was a good inch of snow on the ground, and the temperature was dropping fast. There was also a strong wind which added to the chill. He knew this would mean Sandi would expect a warm and cosy flat when she arrived there just after 10 p.m., so he went to the fire and turned it on. It wasn't the original open fire that had been in the flat when he first bought it. That was long gone. Ed was not someone who could spend time cleaning it out and getting the chimney cleaned. He had had it replaced with a sealed, glass-fronted gas fire. It took minutes to start warming up the room.

She would also be ravenous, and not just for food, he hoped. Ed moved over to the iPad sitting on the coffee table and started up Spotify. He chose a Calvin Harris playlist, not his favourite, but it was good for background music.

As the music played, he went into the kitchen and opened the fridge to remove the pre-made lasagne he had put in there the night before to defrost. It was part of the stockpile of food he had made. One of the things he had picked up at university was living off takeaways and processed foods was not healthy, nor was it cheap. However, he was not one for cooking every night; there were too many parties to attend.

It had got him into the habit of cooking lots of different dishes on a Sunday and freezing them. Then all Ed had to do was reheat them as he needed them. He placed the foiled lasagne in the oven. Ed then brewed a new pot of coffee. Ed wanted something stronger and was tempted to open a bottle of beer, but he didn't want to dull his thought patterns.

As he poured the first mug out, he turned back to the fridge. "Shit," Ed thought. It would have to be black, again. How had he managed to forget the milk? He sent a quick text to Sandi asking her to pick some up.

He moved into the bedroom and took the pad and pen from the bedside cabinet. The room needed tidying up before Sandi arrived. She hated a mess. But it could wait. He still had a couple of hours before Sandi got there. Ed went into the living room and, picking his laptop up off the coffee table and placing his mug in its place, he carried it and the pen and pad over to the sofa, sat down and placed them all beside him.

He turned on the laptop, then after what seemed an age, opened the word document on his desktop. It surprised him that in this day and age computers seemed to open up slower than years ago. He always thought the trillion gigabytes and mega RAM would speed up the things. But to him, even his MacBook seemed slower than his old Windows laptop, and he wondered why he had bought it. But then once it was on and working ...

He picked up his notes; glancing at them as well as the book draft on the screen, he cursed himself again. How could he be expected to finish this? There were more than two weeks of notes that he hadn't used. He had been lazy over these weeks and had concentrated on the draft, trying to get it to work; he wanted the reader to get it, to understand the concept and for it to read well. It was where his greatest fear within him crept in; he felt the idea was crap and that it would read like that, too. He felt he wasn't qualified to write about this subject. He wasn't a historian, he had no knowledge as to whether the facts were correct, but his dreams had been so vivid, and this was going to be a fictional story, wasn't it?

He took a deep breath and reread the book draft.

A little while later Ed was just finishing transcribing the last of his notes on the latest dreams he had had when he heard Sandi open the front door. Ed stood up and, putting the laptop down, walked into the hallway to meet her.

Leaning against the door jamb between the lounge and hallway, he watched as she bent over to take her snow boots off and, not for the first time, wondered why she was with him. He wasn't a short man, but he wasn't tall either. At only 5' 8", Ed was just 2 inches taller than Sandi. He never thought that his looks were great, there were better-looking men in Glasgow. His short blond hair had been residing fast from the age of 18, and his nose was crooked. He wasn't overweight, but he wasn't into all this fitness frenzy that seemed to have hit his generation.

In contrast, Sandi was stunning, with her long legs and slender build. Her hair was long with a gentle curl that she spent hours straightening out. It was the most unusual shade of red, with just the right amount of streaks of auburn in it. She was a keep-fit fanatic and ran at least three times a week, as well as going to the company gym during her lunch breaks. Sandi stood up and began to remove her coat. She smiled at him as he approached her. "How was your day?" she asked as he moved in for a kiss.

"Good," he replied, taking her by the hand and moving back into the lounge. "How about you?" For the next few moments, he listened to her talk about the centre she worked at and the funding cuts she was facing. As she moved to sit down, Sandi saw the laptop there, and as she moved it to the table, it came to life, showing the Jack the Ripper pages open.

"You've been writing?"

He nodded. "But I'm stuck. Do I do some more research into this story, so it is factually correct? Or do I just follow the flow of the dreams?"

When the dreams had started, he had decided to Google them, and he had been shocked at the amount of information that was available. You could find out anything with just a quick tap of a few keys and Google.

Ed had been intrigued to learn about the information and living conditions he had seen in his dreams. Each of the dreams was different, and the ones where he had read articles written in the 1880s, or about visits to the Coroners' Courts, always piqued his curiosity. He had wanted to know whether some of the women spoken about in the newspaper or the courts were Jack's victims.

It was like a dream from the night before when he had read about the body of Martha Tabram being discovered on the first-floor landing of the George Yard Buildings two days before the article was dated. It thought that Martha had met a soldier on Whitechapel High Street and had gone with him into George Yard. Some speculated that she was murdered by Jack the Ripper, back in 1888.

But, the little research he had done made him think that

CHAPTER 3

maybe, just like most of the experts in this field, that the first victim of the Ripper occurred at the end of August. Therefore, Martha was still an unsolved murder. Like all the unsolved killings of this era, there was and still is a lot of debate as to whether or not she was a victim of this wicked man or just a victim of the time.

The records he had read today showed that the murder of Martha was left unsolved and became one of eleven others of the time. These crimes were known as the Whitechapel murders file. It made it almost impossible to tell which of the deaths that occurred during this period (referred to as the Autumn of Terror) Jack had committed and which were possibly copycats or opportunists.

There was one thing that was fact, and that was that Jack the Ripper preyed upon the most unfortunate women who lived in the slums in and around the Whitechapel area. The research that Ed had carried out showed that victims Jack seemed to favour were those that were driven to prostitution to help feed themselves and their families, as well as to help feed their drinking habits. Ed had discovered that these poor women lived in extreme poverty, with overcrowding and homelessness the norm. When looking at the five known victims of this madman, four were in their forties, and the last one, Mary Jane Kelly, was in her mid-twenties.

"Would it hurt to do more research?" Sandi asked. He shook his head; the one thing that any good story could benefit from was excellent research. Ed wrapped his arms around her, kissing her again as he sat down beside her.

"I am starving. Is there any food? Oh. I got the milk." She lifted the carrier bag up that Ed hadn't noticed in his rush to get her into the room and the warmth.

A little later, as they sat on the leather sofa, seemingly watching television and Sandi eating the remainder of the lasagne, it became evident that Ed was unable to concentrate on Stephen Fry trying to educate people on irrelevant and obscure facts. He was engrossed in the book's storyline; trying to think of how to plan it, how could he get it to work, and most importantly would it sell? All his dreams were getting more disturbing and more frightening.

Ed looked at Sandi, deciding to try and move away from the stories in his head. "I saw Weegie today," he told her. "I still don't understand a word he says, but he is such great company. It was such a relaxing afternoon just with him listening to his stories. I would love to write about his life one day. I think I might start recording him so I can get it right."

Sandi laughed. "Most of the homeless out there have the same sad story. Are you going to tell them all? Hey. Good idea, that. You could write a compilation of the homeless stories. You could help one of the charities out with the money you make." She smiled at him. "But, first let's just get this story written before you move on to the next." She pulled the laptop off the table, placed it on her knees and opened a Google page. She then typed in 'The Ripper'. The first result was a Wikipedia page and, on opening it, Sandi started reading it out loud.

4

When she got to the end of the article, Sandi stopped and looked at Ed. They were both shocked at what they were reading. Yes, like most of the population they were aware of the atrocities that occurred towards the end of the 19th century, but this was different, this was about the facts. Ed had skimmed them previously, but this was the first time he had stopped to digest it.

The article they had been reading spoke of the history of the attacks attributed to Jack the Ripper. It was known that the victims were mainly female prostitutes who lived and worked in the slums of the East End of London. They all had their throats cut before he moved onto the abdominal mutilations. Also, in three of the cases, internal organs had been removed. It had led to the notion that the killer maybe had some anatomical or surgical knowledge.

There were only five victims – Mary Ann Nichols, Annie Chapman, Elizabeth Stride, Catherine Eddowes and Mary Jane Kelly – known as the "canonical five", that were linked together. These, as well as the six other killings that occurred over a three-month period in the same area and were unsolved, were the start of the legend that had helped to create the persona of the Ripper.

They were both shocked to find out that there are now more

than 100 theories about the Ripper's identity.

In turn, robbery, violence and alcohol dependency increased. The police estimated that in that year alone, there were around sixty brothels and more than 1,200 women working as prostitutes in the area. The economic problems that accompanied this also caused a steady rise in social tensions. In the latter part of the decade, there were many demonstrations. The public unrest led to police having to intervene.

The article also covered the deaths of Emma Elizabeth Smith to Mary Jane Kelly, with the assumption that Kelly was and still is considered by most to be the Ripper's last victim. It speculated that the crimes ended because of the culprit's possible death, imprisonment, institutionalisation, or emigration.

In the Whitechapel murders file that it wrote about, there was details of another four deaths that happened after the canonical five: those of Rose Mylett, Frances Coles, Alice McKenzie, as well as the Pinchin Street torso.

The author of the piece wrote about the case of "Fairy Fay", but the article is unclear whether the attack was real or a fabrication and, as such, part of the Ripper lore. "Fairy Fay" was the nickname given to the victim allegedly found on Boxing Day, or St Stephen's Day as the Victorians celebrated it, in 1887. The victim had died "after a stake had been thrust through her abdomen". But the records of the time showed no murders in the Whitechapel area around that time and in that manner. It said that Fairy Fay could very well have been confused with the report of the murder of Emma Elizabeth Smith in the Easter and the press confessing the dates. She was killed by a stick or a similar blunt object being shoved into her abdomen.

The web page went on to catalogue the deaths of Annie Millwood, and her admission to Whitechapel Workhouse Infirmary with stab wounds in her legs and lower torso on 25 February 1888. She was later discharged but died from natural causes, aged 38, on 31 March 1888. It then postulated her as the Ripper's first victim, but the attack has never been linked positively to the alleged culprit. Another alleged earlier victim was Ada Wilson, who is said to have survived being stabbed twice in the neck on 28 March 1888. Then there was Annie Farmer, who resided at the same lodging house as Martha Tabram and had reported an attack on 21 November 1888. She had superficial cuts to her throat, though when the doctors examined her it was believed that all the wounds could have been self-inflicted.

When a headless female body was discovered in the basement of the new Metropolitan Police headquarters that was being built in Whitehall, "The Whitehall Mystery" was born. An arm belonging to the same body had previously been found floating in the Thames close to Pimlico, and one of the legs was also discovered buried close to where the torso had been found. However, the other body parts were never recovered, and the body has never been identified. This mutilation was very similar to the Pinchin Street case. The Whitehall Mystery and the Pinchin Street cases could have been part of a series of murders called the "Thames Mysteries" and committed by a single serial killer who was dubbed the "Torso killer". There is still an ongoing debate as to whether Jack the Ripper and the "Torso killer" were the same people or separate serial killers, because the killings occurred in the same area at the same time. But the modus operandi of both killers did differ and police at the time discounted any connection between the two.

The article went on about the police comparing the deaths of John Gill, a 7-year-old boy, who was found murdered in Manningham, Bradford, on 29 December 1888. He had had his legs severed, his abdomen had been opened, with his intestines drawn out, and his heart and one ear removed. There were a lot of similarities between this and the murder of Mary Jane Kelly, which led to a lot of press speculation that the Ripper had killed the young boy, too. It increased in speculation when the boy's employer, William Barrett, was arrested twice for the murder on circumstantial evidence but released both times. To this day, no one else was ever prosecuted.

Then there was Carrie Brown, also known as "Shakespeare" because she was renowned for quoting The Bard's sonnets. The woman was found strangled by her clothing before being mutilated with a knife on 24 April 1891. This murder had occurred in New York, and her remains were found bearing a large tear through her lower body area. There were superficial cuts on her legs and back, but no organs were removed, although an ovary was lying on the bed beside her. It could not be determined if this were done on purpose or just dislodged by accident. The Metropolitan Police were asked to investigate and compare it to the Whitechapel file, but it was eventually ruled out as the same killer. The NYPD and press thought differently, and for a while, they tried to solve the crime with the hope that this would also solve the Whitechapel murders.

The article documented the police performing house-to-house inquiries at the time throughout Whitechapel, as well as all the forensics that were collected and examined. The two of them read that a huge number of suspects were identified, traced and then either considered more carefully or eliminated from the investigation. It is the same pattern that the police still follow today. Throughout the whole inquiry, more than 2,000 people were interviewed, with "upwards of 300" people investigated and eighty people detained.

CHAPTER 4

Among the suspects questioned and sometimes held were butchers, slaughterers, surgeons and physicians because of the manner of the killings. Many contemporary figures, including Queen Victoria herself, believed that the pattern of the murders indicated that the villain was a butcher or cattle drover on one of the cattle boats that sailed between London and mainland Europe. The proximity of Whitechapel and the London Docks made this a possibility. Usually, the boats docked on a Thursday or Friday and departed on a Saturday or Sunday. The police investigated and ruled this out as the dates of the murders did not tie in with any of the boat movements.

One thing they learnt reading the article was about the group called the Whitechapel Vigilance Committee that comprised a group of volunteer citizens from the area, who were patrolling the streets on the lookout for suspicious characters. It had been created because of dissatisfaction with the police effort. Members also petitioned the government to raise a reward for information about the killer, as well as hiring private detectives to help with the questioning of witnesses.

After the pair of them had finished reading it, there was one sure thing that the page concluded, and that was that all five murders were committed by the same person. In the first four, it was apparent that the throat of each woman appeared to be cut from left to right. However, in the last case, owing to the extensive mutilation, it was not possible to say with any certainty in what direction the fatal cut came from, but the forensics on the arterial blood found on the wall showed that it was possibly carried out the same way as the others.

One thing that was known was there is no evidence of any sexual activity with any of the victims. That said, psychologists have speculated that the penetration with a knife and the way they were displayed did indicate that the crimes derived from sexual pleasure. This view was challenged by a few experts, who dismiss such hypotheses as an insupportable supposition.

Because the killings occurred around weekends and public holidays and within a few streets of each other, many have thought that the Ripper was in regular employment and also lived locally. It has also led people to believe that the killer was an educated, upper-class man, such as a doctor or an aristocrat who liked to venture into Whitechapel to enjoy vicarious pleasures.

5

Having digested all that, they moved on to other aspects of the piece and the "Dear Boss" and "Saucy Jack" letters. All the letters written to either the press or the police, or the vigilante organiser George Lusk, were considered hoaxes and fakes. However, one was examined more carefully when Catherine was found three days after that letter's postmark with an ear partially cut off. It was from these letters that the use of the name "Jack the Ripper" gained worldwide notoriety after one of them was published and showed it was signed using that name.

"Okay, so we know that the name 'Leather Apron' was adopted by the press and public to describe the killer. And that Jack was already used to describe another London attacker, 'Spring-heeled Jack', who supposedly leapt over walls to strike at his victims and escape as quickly as he came," Ed said as he read from the laptop. "So we know that the invention and adoption of a nickname for killers is standard media practice. Which is why we have the 'Yorkshire Ripper', 'Boston Strangler' and the like. So that is why this serial killer was so named."

Ed stood up and walked to the window where his packet of Regal sat and, opening the window a fraction, lit up. The snow was still coming down thick and settling on the cars. Ed watched the flakes flutter past the window. He wanted to put his hand out and catch one. It was cold perched on the windowsill, but Sandi wasn't a smoker, so Ed felt guilty lighting up in an enclosed room, especially in the winter, when windows were kept closed. He knew she wouldn't have minded, but Ed also knew that Sandi appreciated his gesture.

Turning to her, he asked: "Am I going mad? I always think of him as me. I know we are two different entities, but I do things in these dreams like him. I know he understands me and I feel he can read my thoughts. But I know nothing about him. I wish I did. I mean I still can't be sure he is a man." Sandi stood up and moved towards him. Ed pushed his arm and cigarette out the window as she moved her hand to his cheek and stroked it.

Sandi didn't understand the fear he had, but she had seen the change in Ed. When he had woken up after the first dream, the bed had been soaked in sweat. She had been woken up by his thrashing about in the early hours of the morning and had moved the chair at the end of the bed and watched him. Sandi had wondered whether she should wake him, but as she had moved towards him to do so, Ed had woken up.

She had jumped back as he gasped for air and looked around the bedroom, trying to figure out where he was. When he had finally pulled himself out of the sleep and had seen her face, he had tried to smile. But as he recited the dream to her, he had cried. For about an hour they had just held each other. She had felt powerless and not able to help him. He was scared.

Ed had changed in the past month, but Sandi couldn't quite put a label on it. He was still the loving man she had met all those months ago, but these dreams seemed to haunt every cell of his body. Ed appeared to be afraid to go to sleep and would almost do anything to defer it. But like everybody, he needed rest to refresh himself, though a month later into the dreams

CHAPTER 5

they wondered how beneficial his sleep was to him.

Sandi had told him to see his GP, but Ed had shrugged it off to start with. However, after about the fourth dream, Ed had made an appointment. The doctor had listened to him and, after a few questions and a few quick tests on his cognitive behaviour, she had told him that, if he was fearful of the dreams, then she could prescribe a sleeping tablet to help relax him; this, she said, may also contribute to having a dreamless sleep.

He had taken her up on this, and on some nights when he had been so tired, he had popped a couple of the tablets. Those nights had been blissfully dreamless, as the doctor had said, but he didn't want to rely on this every night, and he did fear they could be addictive. So he made sure his month's supply lasted longer. Ed had made one decision and that was that he would take them when Sandi stayed over.

The doctor had also suggested that it may help if he went to see a sleep therapist. He had declined this. He didn't feel comfortable going to sleep as part of an experiment. She said she would refer him to see a psychologist if he wished because the doctor said it may help to talk to an expert, and maybe, she suggested, the therapist could help analyse them. However, in her opinion, he was alright, there was no depression or any other type of mental health issue. He just needed to stop smoking and drinking.

As Sandi stood in front of him, he carried on with his thoughts. "He has talked about the preservation of the organs. It is all to do with his education into the origins of these types of people. He says it is to help find a cure to poverty. But I don't believe him. I feel he is hiding his real agenda from me. There is always the great laugh after he talks like this."

"Can I read your notes?" Sandi asked, looking down at

the sofa. She was intrigued to understand what Ed was experiencing.

Ed moved over and picked up his notepad to hand to her. "Remember, these are all my notes of all my dreams. They are not the story, they are just what I write down when I wake up. They are impressions and thoughts as well as things that happened in the dreams." She nodded and turned over the first page. "No, you're better off reading them on the laptop," he said, taking the pad from her, opening up his USB on the laptop and getting the note's document up on the screen. "My handwriting is better on here." He smiled at her.

"From the beginning, these tragedies had been marked by more circumstances and mysterious details that filled everyone who was on the case with horror and dismay. He seems to relish in this misery, and I think he is encouraged by the frenzy his crimes are causing. He watches everybody; he appears to draw from their fear.

"Never before have I experienced so much sexual tension. When I am in Jack's head, the first thing I notice is his hard-on. Is this normal for a serial killer? Should I research this? Maybe it is me that is excited.

"I have read the newspapers of the time as he has; I think I might have to download them here so I can study them better … Can I use them in a book? Or is that plagiarism? That is something I need to check out.

"How many victims did the Ripper mutilate? He has said that there are three so far. He calls the police inept and not able to comprehend his powers. He thinks he should taunt them; he thinks that would be fun. He talks about opening up Detective Inspector Reid just to see how he works. He is quite open about the dissections of the women he has carried out and how he

CHAPTER 5

is learning about the smell of the liver and kidneys. He hopes this will teach him about the human need for alcohol. He says he could tell if a person was a drinker or not by the liver. There was a laugh at this, and he said that the women he had opened up were pissed and that had helped to subdue them. Of course, they drank, and you could smell the whisky on the organs. He also knows if they had borne a child.

"Is he a doctor? I seem to remember a documentary on that and speculation that Jack could have been a doctor or something to do with medicine. But I still think the perpetrator could be female. I know there is the 'hard-on' sensation, but I am only in the brain. The clothing and feeling of skin could be a trick of the mind."

"Is this right?" Sandi asked, looking up at Ed.

Ed nodded. "That is what has scared me the most. Am I just dreaming up a hypothesis for the 'Ripper' story or have I time travelled into his or her mind?"

"I think we need to do some more in-depth research; this could be a great story." She smiled at Ed. "But are you okay to do this?"

"Yes, I think so. Let's get started." He was still perched by the window smoking. His ashtray on the window was overflowing with all the butt ends, so he picked it up to empty it into the bin by the television. He glanced quickly at the screen to see that it still had Stephen Fry talking to his audience and Alan Davies talking about blue whales. He took the control and flicked it off.

"Let me finish your notes then we'll draw up a plan of how this is going to pan out. I'd love some coffee." She looked up at him and watched him move into the kitchen.

6

With Ed in the kitchen, Sandi then started to read the notes now open on the laptop.

"A great wave of nervous, feverish alarm and terror has engulfed London and Jack is enjoying it; he seems to relish in this terror he is creating.

"I am not sure he is the madman as the papers have depicted him, but I could be wrong; he is very guarded about his thoughts. Then there is his boldness in just walking around the streets with his evil cunning way, striking down his victims as he pleases, not leaving the faintest clue as to his identity.

"I have not seen him murder anyone yet and I wonder if I will. Does Jack experiment on poor women for anatomical purposes?? Or is he a madman, who is the irresponsible, bloodthirsty, supernatural person the papers and locals fear?

"No conception can be formed of the motives of his horrible and despicable crimes unless it is reasonable to suppose it was the work of a maniac. Did he seek revenge on this class of women because of some injury he had himself received from one of them? I remember reading these words in the paper. You can hear them spoken in the taverns and street as he walks in between them.

"Do these people understand that they are conversing with the very person who is responsible for their fears and terrors?

CHAPTER 6

"He and I have spoken about the murders, and I know the first one happened on 3 April 1888. The victim was Emma Elizabeth Smith. He is very clear about the date.

"He describes how he watched three men attack her. He is keen to point out that one was a boy. There is a glint in his eye when he says that. He watched them as they attacked her. It was the most thrilling experience of his life, he says. After they had left, he had gone over to look at her in the light of the Bullseye public house. He had gazed into her bleary eyes and smelled her gin-soaked breath; he believed that she would die on that street corner of Brick Lane.

"But he had followed her to her lodgings and then watched her struggle to get to the hospital. The next day, he fretted that the police would come to him and say that maybe she had seen him. But when the incident went unreported and no police officer called, he knew he was free to strike in his own way. He decided that his victims would not survive, that he would ensure they were dead before he left them to the authorities.

"There was a great thrill in his manner when he talked to the police and press. He spoke of the lack of media coverage for Emma Elizabeth; he had watched the people around him shrug it off. 'What else can you expect in Whitechapel with its floating population of criminals and fallen women?' But he wants them to acknowledge his greatness. He wishes to impress them.

"Martha Turner was his first actual victim. On Tuesday, 7 August 1888, she was found lying on her back, her clothing disarrayed, on the first-floor landing of the buildings known as the George Yard Buildings on Commercial Street. It is the one I read about when I woke up from this nightmare.

"He spoke about how he had removed her breasts and laid

them aside. How he had cut her throat. He had left lacerations between her legs with his knife and watched as blood spilt onto the floor leaving a huge stain. He had smiled at these memories.

"He relished in his description of his death blow and the keenness that the head almost severed from her body. It hung loose. It was his way of ensuring she didn't talk. He was not sure how many cuts he made, but he estimated that it was in the thirties on various parts of her body.

"There was his description on how he then opened her up and inserted a pestle into her uterus the same way as he had done with Emma Elizabeth. I was shocked because this was something he knew related to Emma's death. Is that why he had panicked about a possible police visit? He had smiled when he spoke of the jagged wound he had made in the bowels.

"I cringe at his recounting the story; I am horrified that I am talking about this notorious and infamous monster as he recalls his pleasure at the terror he is creating.

"Next, we talked about Mary Ann Nichols and how he killed and mutilated her.

"He left her body in Buck's Row, late at night on 30 August. She had been a heavy woman, and he had dragged her to that spot. He was trying to make an impression. He felt he had been ignored and that the police and press were not taking him seriously; Jack talks about how much his work matters.

"With Buck's Row being a short street, half occupied by factories, half by dwelling houses, he told me that he was sure that the body would be discovered soon and Jack hoped this would instil more fear into these pathetic people, as he called them.

"The brutality of this murder was beyond my conception, and

CHAPTER 6

I don't know if I could do his description justice.

"Her throat had been cut twice. The first cut started under the left ear and ended almost in the centre of her throat. Jack then started the second at this point and moved it towards her other ear. It left a deep and gaping hole, and he took great pleasure in almost severing her head off.

"He has said that if he had had a saw, he would have had to remove it. It would be his sure-fire method of ensuring the death of the women.

"There was a joy that he felt when opening up her abdomen and ultimately exposing all of the internal organs which he had taken his time hanging about her body. He still had part of her bladder and uterus as a keepsake."

"That's all your notes?" she asked, looking up and seeing a coffee in front of her and him at the window smoking.

Ed shook his head. "That's just one night." He stubbed the cigarette out and joined her on the sofa, and he poured the last of the coffee into his cup and drank it. It was just gone midnight, but neither of them was tired. This story seemed to have opened the creative side in each of them. "I woke up this morning from the conversation about Annie Chapman. My biggest problem is that the dreams don't seem to be in order so I was wondering how I could write this. Maybe I can piece it together when it stops, if it stops. I don't want to write it as Jack, but I think I am not doing the story justice writing in the third person. What do you say?"

"I like the narrative," Sandi said, opening Google and searching for newspaper reports of the time as she sipped the new coffee in front of her. Ed had offered her wine, but she had refused after they had agreed they needed clear heads to research this story. She had opened a Word document, and while she read out the newspaper reports and searched archived material for this killer, Ed made notes.

7

It was midday before they crawled out of bed. Ed and Sandi had finally given up research for the story at five that morning. Both were buzzing with the information they had gleaned, but with all that information and the coffee they had consumed, the cry for sleep was inevitable. Ed had taken one of his tablets before retiring; he wanted to sleep and it seemed the tablets had given him that.

"I knew there was a reason I'd gone to university," Ed said, feeling rather pleased with himself. The story seemed to be forming well in his head, thanks to the fresh eyes of Sandi and the good night's sleep he'd had. It wasn't all there, but then the dreams were still incomplete, too. Yes, he knew this was going to be a rehash of an old and rather over-told story, but he felt his tale was going to add a new dimension to it. Ed, in a sense, had the advantage of seeing the killings from the mind of Jack. He set his feet on the coffee table and opened the laptop, ready to start searching again.

"So, are we going again?" Sandi said as she walked into the room with a plate of bacon sandwiches and a fresh pot of coffee. To her, it was good to see Ed energised.

"Well, you have to admit, up to now all I seem to have been doing is thumping along with no direction. I have been worrying so much about going to sleep and not dreaming, but with these tablets I feel I could get this done.

"You know that to write a good book you have to write around 10,000 words a day; I only got about 1,500–2,000 words written down so far. I know that's not a lot, but with all the notes we've got, that should bump that up to about 20,000, I reckon. I just need the ending. A good book should be around 40–70,000. I am not sure I could write that much."

"What's next?" She laughed as she sat next to him and pecked his cheek. To her this was exciting and, having no work for the next two days, Sandi was looking forward to this different type of challenge. She had her degree in English literature, but her chosen career meant it was unused.

He smiled. "Well, I think we need to get the murders sorted out chronologically. Do we just focus on these deaths that are said to be Jack's or all the alleged ones, too? I mean, that would be all eleven unsolved murders of that time. That is a big story and a lot of research."

"Let's just concentrate on the ones you are dreaming about; I think they are the important ones, for now. If we need to look at others, we can."

Nodding his head, he started reading the notes and text they had made the night before. "Okay, Martha Tabram. She was the one I started this dreaming with; it was her newspaper article I read. But she is not one of the canonical five, is she?" Sandi shook her head. "However, I have to keep her in the book. She must have some connection, or why did I dream about her? That said, her death was just weeks before Mary's."

"Okay, I agree. There is a reason why you dreamt about the article, and we will find out. Maybe Jack can tell you?" Sandi smiled at Ed.

They spent a while discussing it and writing notes ready to use in the book. Ed then started creating a plan of how the book would read. But he had no ending, that worried him; it was going against how he had been taught to write. But he hoped that when he had fully rested, he could resume the dreams.

His plan started with Martha. She was the one who had started this all off. He then made notes about Mary Ann Nichols, who was next and considered the first of the canonical five. She had been discovered in a gateway in Buck's Row on 31 August that year.

It was about a week later that Annie Chapman had been found in the backyard of Number 29 Hanbury Street on 8 September. It was this murder that seemed to push the unease that had been bubbling away in the area since the two deaths in August. For the first time, panic was felt on the streets.

There had been speculation in the press that this could have been the reason there was an absence of several weeks before Jack returned to the streets. However, on 30 September, he claimed two victims, and both within an hour of each other. The first casualty was Elizabeth Stride, and it seems very likely that Jack was interrupted in the act of her murder.

These killings were dubbed the "night of the double event".

Elizabeth Stride was Swedish and was found murdered with her throat cut from ear to ear and again her head almost decapitated, but she wasn't mutilated like the others. Ed thought this seemed relevant and wondered what had happened to stop this madman going further?

"According to this report she was also known as 'Hippy Lip Annie'," Sandi said. "The body was still warm when it was found; Jack must have been spooked."

"So, that would account for the next woman discovered that night, although it was only fifteen minutes later, yet there is a report that says it was an hour later. That's strange. Okay, let's compare the two women. You do Elizabeth, and I'll look up Catherine."

As they read into the events of the night, it was clear that the second victim was Catherine Eddowes and her body was found in Mitre Square at 1.45 a.m. Her injuries were absolutely horrific, and it looked like Jack had taken away a trophy of his crime. Her kidneys were missing.

The rest of the afternoon was taken up with the two of them chatting about these two women and their murders on 30 September.

"So, this could be why he never mutilated her. If you think about it, you can see it. He has cut her throat, first. That would stop her from shouting and alerting someone to what was going on. Then he has to ready himself to carry out the incision on her abdomen. But then what happened? Does he hear the cart approach? Maybe he jumped into the shadows. We know it would have been dark around there so it would have been easy to hide. The only problem is why didn't Diemshutz have a lantern? I thought a man on carts in that area would have had a lantern. It was dark ..." Ed let the words trail. There were so many questions, and neither of them seemed to have the answers.

Sandi picked up a report about Diemshutz and started commenting on it. "I love the sentiment that if Diemshutz had acted differently, then history may never have known about Jack the Ripper as the man in the shadow, the unknown assailant. Well, no, he wouldn't have been as widely known, maybe. He may not have held this rather macabre infamy that we speak of." Sandi smiled. "Just think, this man could have been standing feet away from a monster and, listen, he thought it was his wife, so instead of raising the alarm he walked into the building to check she was okay. Jack must have been laughing at his good luck. It was a perfect getaway."

"But he must have been enraged that he had not been able to complete his mission. That's got to be why Catherine was killed. I can tell you this is not a sane man."

"It says here that Elizabeth had no money on her when she was found, so it's likely that her night's takings, and we know she was seen with three men that night, were taken. Is it something Jack would have done? Or was it stolen by someone else before her death?" She took in a breath as she watched Ed get up to have a cigarette. "What if she wasn't a Ripper victim, just an unlucky prostitute that was killed by a client and robbed? He could have used the Jack terror to cover his tracks."

Ed was looking out the window, thinking about this. It had stopped snowing, but there had been a considerable amount that had come down overnight and into the morning. As the light was fading, he watched the people on the street all huddled up in hats, gloves and coats, plodding through the snow as they were coming home from work.

"No, I think this was Jack. There may have been issues with what hand he used, and whether it was from behind or in front, but I can say that all the killings I have seen have been committed by the same man. He knows what he is doing. So if the police think this was Jack ..." He trailed off.

Ed turned back to face Sandi and sat beside her on the sofa. "Okay, the last victim was Mary Jane Kelly. She died on 9 November, yes?" Sandi nodded. "I read somewhere, last night, that there was speculation about her death and some people believed that she was a copycat killing. And the only reason given was that she was killed inside."

As Ed lit another cigarette, he carried on with the thoughts going through his head. "He's smart, don't forget that, and I know he enjoys watching people and following them. Look up John Eddleston. I think that's the name. I remember seeing an essay by him last night about Mary Jane Kelly not being a copycat murder as many speculate. There is another article I printed off by a Dan Norder that is good." He looked at her as her nimble little fingers typed in the names. "Are you hungry? I was thinking of ordering in."

8

"I've meant to ask ..." Sandi was sitting in front of him eating pizza. They had decided, that given the hour and the fact that they hadn't got much food in, that it may have been prudent to go out and eat. They needed a break, and seeing that afternoon had now become evening, it seemed a good idea. They quickly showered and donned their warm clothing – something the Scottish people did well; they knew how to dress for the weather.

The pair then walked, hand in hand, the short distance to the taxi rank and took a cab to the city centre. Having opted for Papa John's, they were now sitting there mulling over their findings and tucking into the large pepperoni pizza in front of them. Sandi had ordered a glass of red wine, and he had a beer.

"Why did you decide to write this? Is it just because of the dreams or have you always been fascinated by this story?"

"No, this is not my type of subject. I find it hard to comprehend that people can do this sort of thing to each other." He looked at her, "I am a softy really. I hate violence. That said, if I were to pick a subject to write about, then it would be along these lines: This genre sells. You only have to look at films. People like it." He shook his head. "No, people are obsessed with the dark side of life. And that means that horror and gloom are what the reading public wants, too. I mean if you look at Amazon and the bestsellers, then as well as the guru books, you are sure to see a thriller or crime book in the top ten." He said between mouthfuls, "Seriously, I hate those types of stories. I do prefer romance and wonder."

She looked at him as he spoke, not so shocked at this. Yes, she had loved that if they watched a film, it would be a 'chick flick', but she did enjoy some of the crime thrillers, and though they had watched them together, she now understood his apathy to them.

"It's just the idea seems to have opened up the floodgates within me, and I can see the story working. I am not sure exactly where in the hell this story is going, but that will come, I hope, in time. What is important is to convey the story in the best way I can. I hate the Jack the Ripper idea, and I definitely am not a Ripperologist. I didn't even know what one was before reading that bit in Rumbelow's classic *Jack the Ripper: The Complete Casebook*," he continued.

"Weren't you surprised that he could find no mention of Israel Schwartz..." Sandi started to ask, and Ed reached over and placed a finger on her lips. She understood the gesture straightaway. Maybe they should just enjoy their night out.

He knew she was staying over until the Sunday, when she was back at work. He lifted his head and called the waitress over to settle the bill. They stood and walked out into the cold night and started walking back towards his house.

"How about going to Òran Mór for a nightcap?" he asked as they walked down the street. Òran Mór was where they had met. She had been out on a hen party for a friend, and he had arranged to meet his friend Jimmy there. He was downing his second pint when she had tripped and spilt her cocktail down his back.

CHAPTER 8

He had turned ready to hit the culprit, only to come face to face with Sandi; she had the most horrified look on her face and was close to tears. "I'm soo sooorrry, sorry. Oh dear. Sorry." She had slurred. Her speech was very slow as if she was frightened of mispronouncing the words. "I'm on a hen party and think I may have had too much drink." He had just looked at her for what seemed like an age before she smiled at him. "Are you okay?" she asked.

"Yes, yes, fine." Then, looking down at her empty glass, asked: "Can I get you a drink?"

"Water ... No, coffee. Please."

He had ordered the drinks, and they walked over to a spare table by the door and with his wet back forgotten they had talked non-stop. Sandi's friends had looked for her as they had left to move on to the next pub, but had missed seeing her in the corner chatting away to Ed.

She was sobering up fast while talking to Ed; they seemed to be oblivious to the whole room. Even when one of her friends had tried to phone her, she hadn't heard it, she hadn't even seen it light up on the table in front of her. It was only when Ed had got up to get another drink, she noticed the missed call and just texted them that she would see them at the wedding and she was fine.

Unknown to Ed, his friend Jimmy had walked in, just as Ed walked back to the table with the refilled glasses. Jimmy had gone up to the bar and ordered a pint while scanning the room for his pal. When he caught sight of him chatting with a beautiful redhead girl in the corner, he had smiled to himself and quickly finished his pint, before moving over and patting Ed on the shoulder, smirking at him before leaving and going on to another pub.

When the bar had finally called closing time at midnight, they left hand in hand heading back to his place and had never looked back. The only regret was that he hadn't persuaded her to move in permanently. Yes, she was at his place whenever she wasn't working. But her job meant shift work, and Sandi felt it was unfair to subject him to that. Though the real reason was she felt he could support himself and that when the money did get low, he had a position in the printing firm to fall back on, but that would mean him moving back to Surrey.

She wasn't keen on leaving Glasgow. It was her hometown and, at the age of 22, having just completed her degree the year before, felt it was not the right time to leave. Having only been working for nine months, it wasn't something she wanted to think about. She needed to get some experience behind her before she could think of moving to England. So, while there was a chance that he could make it as a writer, she would stand by him. She did worry about his dreams and this book, but she trusted him.

They got out of the cab and crossed the road to go into the Waitrose to pick up some cigarettes before going to the pub. The place was still busy, considering the weather and the fact it was a Wednesday night. However, as they walked inside and towards the bar, it was apparent that there were also a few Christmas parties going on. There would be some sore heads tomorrow, both of them thought, seeing the revellers at the bar.

"What are you having?" Ed asked as they pushed their way to the bar. "Red wine, please," she almost shouted back.

He looked over to the seat that they seemed to think of as their own and noticed it was free. He nudged Sandi and watched as she walked towards it.

CHAPTER 8

He was enjoying this newly found zest for writing. It had always been a passion, but this was the first time a story seemed bigger than a few pages he would get ready to recite to the family at Christmas. He also felt moved that Sandi was there to help him. She had gone some way in contributing to restoring his faith in his basic ability to write down his dreams into a coherent narrative. He knew he was good at writing. Ed had been able to enthral his audiences in the past as he had narrated his short stories to his readers. Now he had to show he could write a novel.

The relationship between the two of them had confused her friends. Yes, they understood her desire to succeed in her career, how Sandi had planned out her career path. But with Ed, she seemed to accept his laziness, his inability to want to work. They saw him as bone idle. She had told them about his situation. Sandi had explained about his windfall and desire to move away from his family, but, because Sandi still had problems understanding the whole thing, they too had not comprehended the need within Ed to find himself.

As a result, they shied away from him, and this was one of the reasons she would not move in. Sandi wanted Ed to prove his worth to himself as well as the world. This time together, the research they were doing was bringing out her creative side, and she was relishing it. Yes, it had only been a short period since leaving her education, but it was nice to help to create a story.

When he came over to join her, he had a bottle of wine and two glasses as well as two generous drams. "To keep away the cold," he said as he handed her one and chinked it before they both swallowed the amber nectar and felt it warm them up as it moved down their throats and into their stomachs.

"Good call." She reached over and planted a kiss on his lips.

"Okay, what are we going to discuss? The book or us?" He watched her face turn quickly towards him and couldn't help but laugh. "The book it is. I know we're perfect, but you are going to have to make your mind up about a proposal."

"I told you I would have an answer for you before Hogmanay." He nodded in assent. He knew he had taken a chance asking her to marry him the week before. He had hoped that marriage would change her mind and she would move in as well as it make her see he was serious about them and their life together. They were young, but they fitted together. He knew she was going to say yes, but this waiting was her way of earning respect from his parents and family without a ring on her finger, and he loved her all the more for that.

"So the book. Do you remember who the main suspects were?" she asked as she poured the wine into their glasses. They spent the bottle of wine and two chasers looking up suspects and trying to decide which one could be in Ed's head.

9

"So he knew you had been drinking? That's interesting," Sandi stated as they sat on the sofa with coffee in their hands. It was still dark outside, but the dream that night had shocked Ed so much he didn't think he would sleep again that night. The images of the dream were still going around in his head, and Ed wanted to write them down before they dispersed. He also needed to smoke.

"Yes, but it wasn't just that that frightened me. It was strange, but Jack seems to understand me. He was probing me and asking about the things he could see in my mind. Thankfully Jack didn't comprehend cars or the things that we see around us now, but he could see them. He kept asking questions about my life. He knows I live in Glasgow. He …" He saw Sandi's puzzled look and told her about his thoughts and how he had been questioned about Ed's life. However, it had scared Ed, and he felt that it was not right to explain modern life to Jack.

He put down his cup and moved over to the window, and when he had opened it, he lit up another Regal. He looked out into the night, watching the snow fall again. Tomorrow was going to be horrendous for the commuters. Yes, it was not unusual to have snow in December, just not this much. "I think the most frightening thing was he knew I had been drinking and he did not like that." Ed shuddered. "I do wish I had taken a tablet last night."

Looking back out the window at the cold conditions, he suddenly wondered how Weegie and the others were. Yes, they had the temporary shelter, but it may have been full. He had decided to go into the city in the morning and check on Weegie and possibly buy him and some of the others a good hot breakfast each.

The two of them sat there in the front room, drinking coffee and Ed smoking, waiting for dawn to finally give way to a full morning, albeit with the sun hidden behind the snow clouds and the streets still all white. They decided to go and hunt out Weegie and treat him to breakfast.

The city centre was crowded with mothers shopping and having the added burden of the children home because of school closures. There were also a lot of people taking advantage of a snow day to catch up on Christmas shopping.

The only conversation that seemed to occupy both Sandi and Ed was that of Jack, as they sat at the table outside their favourite café. It was broken by the familiar voice of their friend.

"I rite ye this, guid tae see ye." They turned to Weegie, him shuffling towards them. He was dressed in the same as he had been in on Tuesday and his beard seemed to have grown. His hat was pulled down over his face, and he was wearing a pair of glasses.

Sandi stood and moved towards him, holding her arms out and waiting for a customary hug, but his hands stayed in his pockets and with a shrug he said: "Sorry stay braw oan

CHAPTER 9

th' hands." This didn't deter her, and she wrapped her arms around him. After a moment, she pulled away, slipping beside him and hooking her arm through his.

"Breakfast, I think. Please join us. And I will not accept a no from you." She guided Weegie to their table and Ed. There were just a few people sitting outside, too, and nobody looked up as they sat down again. The area was covered by an awning, and there were many gas heaters dotted about, giving off enough heat to make it bearable.

They ordered coffee and 'The full works' with link sausages, square sausage, two rashers of bacon and eggs, scrambled or fried. This was served with a portion of fried mushrooms, a round of black pudding, potato scones and beans. There were also six slices of toast to be brought out with it.

While they sat there waiting for the food to appear, they chatted about the weather and asked how Weegie was faring with it.

"Och. Th' shelter is stoatin. Thaur ure naw beds thaur, which is guid in thes weaither. An' th' scran is fair. Ah, cannae grumble. It's braw tae be wi' friends an' th' staff ur guid."

"They caur but dornt try tae change us. Hoo hae ye tois bin?"

"We're alright. Been looking into Ed's book and coming up with some interesting things." She then proceeded to bring him up to date with all the research they had done. "But I think we need a break, and to talk about something different; tell us a story." She smiled at Weegie and waited as he thought.

"Ah. Hae ye ever heard ay 'the beast ay Birkenshaw?'" They both shook their heads. "Nae it was a bit af a time aga. His real name was Peter Thomas Anthony Manuel an' he hanged fur his crimes oan th' eleventh ay July in '58." Weegie looked at their faces. He enjoyed it when he could impart a bit of his knowledge onto others. He narrated the story in his broad accent that Sandi had to translate occasionally.

They both listened to Weegie talk about Peter Thomas Anthony Manuel, who was a US-born Scotsman convicted of murdering seven people across Lanarkshire and southern Scotland over a two-year span. It was also believed he killed two others, but the cases had to be dropped through lack of evidence. Just before his arrest, Manuel gained the nickname "the Beast of Birkenshaw" by the media. He was also one of the last prisoners to die on the Barlinnie gallows.

He was born in 1927 in New York City and had moved back to Britain, with his parents, in 1932. They actually moved to Birkenshaw, in North Lanarkshire. It was said that he was bullied at school, because of his accent and manner. About the same time, he was also known to the police as a petty thief. But it was when he was 16 that his crimes escalated; he served nine years for sexual assault. However, the conviction was on the work carried out by the police, not DNA, as it would have been today. In 1955 he was cleared of rape. He had conducted his own defence, something that is not heard of today and, because it was only his word against the victims, he won.

But even though he was known to the police for his other crimes and was their prime suspect in the horrific murders, they still couldn't pin them on him.

One of the biggest problems the police came up against was that it is quite common for people, when they find out that someone they have known for years has committed a crime, to be surprised and find it hard to believe that this 'average' person they knew could do such a thing. Even Peter's father thought his son was innocent and this was the reason he offered himself up for the murders.

CHAPTER 9

Weegie went on to say that this was the problem with most serial killers – they have the ability to behave in a rational manner, which is one of the reasons they can be hard to capture. Today it is easier with DNA and FBI profiling, but that is a new concept. Police didn't have this luxury four or five decades ago. Can you imagine the problems in Victorian London? Fingerprinting was not used in the police investigation until recently. Weegie continued as the big plates of food were placed in front of them.

"Sauces?" the waiter asked to the three of them and walked away as they all shook their heads.

Weegie continued talking. "In that auld days, th' idea that someone's fingerprints wur used in connection wi' th' crime wis nae polis procedure. Sae, ye kin forgoat a' this CSI knowledge o' th'day."

The food was hot and going down fast, but it didn't deter the talking. "'twas a' aboot witnesses 'n' a policeman's hooter. Th'day we blether aboot profiling. 'n' aye, ah dae aye read th' papers, ah kin be a bin howker, bit a'm aye alive. This is ma choice; ah cuid gang 'n' fin' a steid tae settle doon in. Bit a'm a bawherr auld in th'tooth fur that, 'n' ah wid lassy th' buzz ah git fae th' streets."

"How long have you been on the streets?" Ed asked.

"Ah reckon 30 years. Ah can't be sure." He was just finishing up his food and looking forward to digesting it all with a cup of tea and a roll up.

"How do you know this story of Manuel?" Sandi asked.

10

It was the last of Sandi's last day before she went back to work, and they chose to make the most of it and set out on a somewhat challenging walk to the Glasgow Botanic Gardens in the snow. It is an amazing collection of several glasshouses and, most notably, the Kibble Palace. The gardens had been created in 1817 and run by the Royal Botanic Institution of Glasgow. The gardens were originally used to hold concerts and other events of the time and, in 1891, the gardens were incorporated into the Parks and Gardens of Glasgow.

They spent the afternoon looking around the Kibble Palace with its wrought iron-framed glasshouse. In 2004, a restoration programme had been initiated to repair the building, and it opened to the public in November 2006.

The couple spent the afternoon working around the plants and forgetting about the book for a few hours. They then walked up to the One Devonshire Gardens for an early evening meal. After an enjoyable afternoon and evening, Ed left Sandi at her flat so she could ready herself for work the next day.

When Ed made it back home, he pondered over something that Weegie had touched on: how often serial killers went unapprehended. It seemed impossible to believe, but when he looked into it, he was shocked to discover that a lot of serial killers had got away with murder. He learnt that even today,

CHAPTER 10

with technological advancements, there are still the 'invisible' killers out there who are always watching and waiting for their next kill.

Their persona helped them hone the art of picking the right place, victim and time. DNA, profiling and the like didn't always ensure the capture and conviction of these killers. One of the techniques he read they used was preparation. The perpetrators of these crimes will plan and stalk the victim. They will check everything and will not attack till they are sure that the offence can be committed safely. They are highly organised people and will always ensure they are one step ahead of the police. They will wear gloves and clothing as well as masks that help prevent skin transfer and leaving fingerprints. They will wear a hat to avoid hair contamination.

It is known that these predators will use chemicals to help clean up after themselves. Ed wondered about this as he had always thought that blood could remain on clothes and the like even if they are cleaned and bleached. However, as he researched, it became apparent that although it is impossible not to leave any evidence behind, if it degrades before being collected, then it cannot be used.

It seemed that being patient and taking extraordinary measures has helped these killers. Some will target victims who are not likely to draw attention if they go missing. The type of victim they select are strangers and possibly in the ethnic minority. It is rare that someone in this group will get the same attention as a Caucasian victim.

So today's serial killer could pick any of the illegal immigrants in the country, and nobody would bat an eyelid. Ed wondered just how many victims there were out there that had ended up as prey to these psychopaths? Hiding in the shadows waiting for the next immigrant, knowing they would be unreported by loved ones, who were reluctant to come forward, even if they had seen anything suspicious. There were also those unfortunate victims that no one notices disappearing at all.

In an article, Ed read it said that female serial killers were often smarter than males. The reason the article gave was that female serial murderers use covert murder methods that make it harder to detect. He remembered many stories of nurses asphyxiating a patient close to death, and this made the crime hard to detect. Most of the time it would have been attributed to natural causes. Female offenders are more likely to target very vulnerable victims and at the same time using methods that are harder to detect.

There was no doubt in his mind that Jack was a man, even if people speculated otherwise. It was a fact that one of the victims, Polly, was said to be a large woman, possibly too heavy for a woman to carry. Unless she had help? Ed pondered for a moment, but no, that wouldn't have been possible. He knew the police had made a lot of errors in their hunt for Jack, but a duo was more likely to have been caught, or rather, he felt that the police would have apprehended the pair; errors on the killer's part would have led to this.

Ed was intrigued to read even today the police make mistakes. Not all of the time, but there are cases where crime scenes become contaminated before the collection of the evidence. Some predators will select crime scenes in remote areas where the police may not be used to handling these sorts of murders, thus leading to mistakes being more likely to happen and the killer getting away with their crimes.

He went to bed, alone, pondering the life of a serial killer, and tablet free.

CHAPTER 10

Ed was up early the next morning; it was always the same after having Sandi stay for a few days. When she wasn't there, the bed was a lonely place and cold. He sent her a quick sloppy text and proposed to her again. She replied with a smiley face and told him she would be back in a few days. They also arranged to meet up for lunch the next day before her shift started.

After showering and dressing, he sat down to spend the rest of the morning going through the timeline that Sandi had put together for him. It was good to have something there to help unscramble the dreams and order them. There was one thing that was for sure – these visions were not in chronological order.

He also realised that this story was not the easiest to tell. Yes, Ed could write his story about going to the inquests of these women, he could speak of the women and their deaths, and he could try and explain what Victorian England or, more precisely, about the slums of Whitechapel, but would that be adequate? Would the story have the legs to sell, or would it just be one of those pitiful attempts at making it as a writer? It scared him that he was not good enough to do this.

He had been sitting there with all his notes and decided that he needed to start writing. The notes he had made were not sufficient to see if it was working, and last night's dream seemed to be the beginning of the story ...

11

These nightmares are now getting worse, and tonight I stood in that dark alley, shocked and unable to get the horrific images out of my head. That poor woman attacked in front of me, and I was powerless to stop it. However, even with all the horror of it, I was not able to tear my eyes from the scene in front of me.

I could hear her crying and screaming as they subjected her to that brutal beating and rape. I know that it is something I will never forget. The thugs, no, animals; but even that is not the right word. They were jeering and laughing. The youngest of the four was no older than 13 or maybe 14; the boy was leering at the semi-naked body lying on the ground with his trousers around his ankles. He then bent down and thrust himself into her. I watched in horror as the others took their turn – there is no feeling of hurrying; it's as if the world has stopped caring and the folks in the home around the alley turned a blind eye.

As the men finished and moved off, I watched the woman as she tried to get up and right herself, but at this moment she was powerless. The attack had left her lying on the cold, damp ground. Slowly, the body that I am watching the horror from moved towards her. I have discovered in my waking hours that this is Emma Smith, and as we cross the cobbles and avoid the piles of dung, I can feel the excitement rising within me, the need to see her. I am unsure why I should feel this. I am horrified at the thought that this woman was exciting me.

I remember the feeling I had felt just a short while before this attack, when she had been standing outside the church; the gang had approached and she had crossed over to almost where I stood. To my hiding place. I had moved further into the shadows to stop her from spying me. Emma was that close I could smell her; that nasty, dirty and musty aroma I was growing accustomed to. One of the men had crossed the street to face her and had spoken her name. She had moved back, and I had panicked just for a moment that we had been seen but, to my delight, or rather his, she had followed the man back to the others, and I had listened to her explain that she had nothing to give them. She had spent her last few pennies on her rent and food.

I had felt myself smile at the group laughing and start the attack. Now just a few moments later I am looking down at Emma's broken body. But that scared me, too. Why was I enjoying this? Or why was the body I am trapped in enjoying it?

Up to now, all I had ever done was watch the people around me as they carried on their pathetic lives, I had sat and watched them go to work and return hours later. I knew from history that London's East End was notorious for its extreme deprivation. It was hugely overpopulated and characterised by the very depressing living conditions, such as the sweatshop industries, poverty and disease. It was a place that was feared with trepidation by many outsiders. In the papers, the middle-class described this "Outcast London" as a foreign country and its inhabitants as a strange race of people. Some even compared it to living next to hell.

It was on the second night I realised I was standing with someone or, to put it more accurately, I was in another person's body. So, it was not me standing on the corner watching the stevedores at St Katherine's dock, struggling to unload the ship in port, but someone else, with me looking through his eyes.

I was trapped, unable to communicate with the people in the street. I had tried to talk to the other person in the last two encounters, but either he wasn't able to hear me or didn't want to communicate. I felt like I was a silent observer and now I was scared as well. I wanted to know what was happening. Even just ask who he was and why I was there. All I heard was laughing now and as I looked down at the woman on the floor in front of me ...

It wasn't the first time I had heard his laugh, that was one of the reasons I knew I wasn't alone. He had laughed when we had come across the "High Rip" gangs patrolling the Whitechapel area and as they walked towards Emma, who was standing there waiting for her next client. History had taught me that these types of groups were renowned for extorting money from prostitutes and other downtrodden women of the age in return for offering them the protection of the group. But as so often happened, as I had watched with Emma, the poor women had little or no money and were still brutally attacked.

Emma was laying there after the men had finished with her and we were looking at her bleed; I sensed that he was watching and praying for her to die. In what seemed an unspoken manner, he told me that he wanted to see what happened at the moment of death. With her skirt raised, you could see, as well as smell the blood, that coppery taste you got in your mouth. The odour was tingling my nose as it left her body and I wanted to pinch my nostrils to stop the smell enticing the weird sensations in me.

For what seemed like ages we stood over her as we watched

CHAPTER 11

the bruises around her eyes as they developed. We moved around the body, and I noticed that her right ear was torn and bleeding. Her face was bloody, too. It was the strangest sensations I have ever experienced; I was bending over her and using a gloved hand to examine her wounds. I find myself smiling at the thoughts of how the body could endure so much pain and trauma, but still survive.

I knew that Emma was still alive and that the attack had not and would not kill her tonight as she opened her eyes and looked at me for a moment. I was frightened for just a moment and moved away from her to the shadows again. She pushed herself up to a sitting position, before getting to her feet. I had wanted to go back to her to put an arm out to help, but was prevented; this was not allowed.

Then Emma started the long walk – almost crawl – to George Street. As she got closer to her address, I was amazed to see that she was still walking on her two legs, slowly, but she was walking with such great determination. It had been while making her way through these depraved streets, full of carnage and rotting food and her faltering to catch her breath, she had removed her shawl from her shoulders and placed it between her legs to soak up the blood that was visibly flowing down her skirt.

She had approached her lodgings, and I could see the sun was close to dawning. Two women were standing in the doorway, talking and watching her, almost laughing. It was when they saw her stumble that they rushed to her aid. I watched from across the road, hidden in the shadows of alleyways and passages, and noticed the astonished looks the women gave each other. They started screaming and shouting for help, but nobody came. Nobody cared enough to help.

One asked Emma how she managed even to get home. Emma shook her head and mumbled things. I can't hear what she is saying, and it became apparent that the women probably didn't understand, either. They moved closer to her to try to listen. Then, just as easily as that, the two women almost scooped her up and rushed her to the London Hospital, even with Emma fighting them all the way.

She was not going willingly. I wish I could have helped. I also wish I could erase the images in my head.

I could only assume and hope that once inside the hospital she was seen by a house surgeon. I was hoping that she would survive, that she could identify the men and they would get the punishment they deserved. This thought gave me the feeling of fear within me. This body I am trapped in actually feared something, and I suddenly realised that the stranger I was caught up in feared that Emma would identify him.

12

I was back in the Whitechapel area and sat on wooden benches spread out in this cold, damp-smelling hall. One of the women I had seen helping Emma to the hospital was standing up in a makeshift witness box.

There to the left of her were twelve men sitting on the same type of bench I sat on. All of them were dressed in suits and were writing things down as the woman spoke.

There was a table to the right of the woman with a stern-looking man wearing a robe with a clerk next to him, again taking notes. Around the room, I could see what I assumed to be reporters scribbling on pads, ready to get this story into the morning editions. The rest of the benches were taken up with people of the area, who had come in to learn the truth about their neighbour and how she had died. Or maybe they were here in the hope that it was warmer than the streets?

Mrs Mary Russell was the deputy keeper of a common lodging-house, where Emma lived, and yes, she said she had known Emma for about two years. On the evening before the attack, she had seen Emma as she left home at around seven o'clock. Mary had not seen Emma before her return at about four or five the next morning. Emma had been in a dreadful state. Her face and head were severely injured, and one of her ears had nearly been torn off.

Emma had told Mary and the friend that she was with that she had been set upon and robbed of all her money, although it wasn't much. Emma also complained of pains in the lower part of her body. There was blood all down her skirts. The two women had taken Emma to the hospital, and as they made their way to the London Hospital, they had passed through Osborne Street, where the attack occurred. Emma had pointed out the exact spot to the women, and there was blood on the path. The two women had asked Emma to tell them what had happened and she had told them that there had been three men, but Emma had not been able to describe them because she was too weak.

At the hospital, Mr George Haslip, who was the next witness, and a house surgeon there, stated that upon admission it was clear that Emma had been drinking, but she wasn't intoxicated. He went on to say that there was bleeding from a head and ear injury. There were also other injuries of a "revolting nature".

The doctor went on to say that he discovered that Emma was suffering from a rupture of the peritoneum, or the abdominal wall, which he suspected had been perforated by some blunt instrument and would have had to be inflicted with considerable force to cause her injuries. She had been coherent enough to tell him about the assault. He was said to say that her death had ensued on Wednesday morning after the attack and was a result of peritonitis.

The next witness to speak was Margaret Hayes, who lived at the same address as Emma. She had said that she had seen Emma in the company of a man at the corner of Farrant Street and Burdett Road. The woman had gone on to describe this man as a very well- dressed gentleman in a dark suit, and he wore a white silk handkerchief around his neck. She went on

CHAPTER 12

to say he was of medium height.

I could feel the mind I was within become more alert; his head seemed to crane to catch her words. When asked if she would recognise him again, she declined. I could feel Jack as he sat up straighter to listen to the next witness.

The police officer that came to the stand next stated that he had no other official information on the subject and he was only aware of the case through the daily papers. I was shocked that the police didn't know that this woman had died so horribly. He had questioned the constables on the beat after reading about the death, but none of the men knew anything about the matter. If this had happened in my time, it would have been reported by the doctor, on Emma's admission, but in this time, nobody cared.

The coroner summed the whole case up in a few sentences and Emma Smith's life was likened to "barbarous murder". He could not imagine a more brutal and dastardly assault, and he instructed the jury to record their verdict at once rather than adjourning the case to another date in the hope of having more evidence brought before them. The jury agreed and returned a verdict of "Wilful murder by some person or persons unknown".

It was the press of the time which linked Emma Smith's death to the Whitechapel murders, a series of unsolved murders that all happened in the area around the last two or three years of that decade. The Metropolitan Police had filed eleven crimes under this title. Today, most experts believe that Emma's death was just a result of random gang violence. At this time in history, Whitechapel was home to many notorious gangs who patrolled the streets harassing any unfortunate women such as Emma and, in most cases, their only crime was demanding money in exchange for "protection". The original "pimps".

In the next dream, I knew that we were in a different month. It wasn't as cold as the other time. That said, I noticed that the rain had just stopped and the roads were damp. It only added to the atrocious smells. If the streets around London had this problem today, then the mayor would be trolled on Twitter, but the people milling around seemed unaware of the stench.

I was standing on the corner of Commercial Road and Fournier Street, as the street signs on the buildings told me. The body I inhabited pulled a paper out from under his arm and opened it up. Once he found the page he wanted, he folded it to read it.

Yesterday afternoon, the article read, "Mr G. Collie R, deputy coroner for the South-Eastern Division of Middlesex, opened an inquiry at the Working Lads' Institute, Whitechapel Road. It was in respect to the death of a woman who had been found on Tuesday last, with 39 stabs wounds to her body. She had been discovered in George Yard Buildings, Whitechapel."

I was shocked at this and wondered what the date was. I glanced up to the top of the page and noticed it was Friday, 10 August 1888. I racked my brain to think about this date, but I knew that this wasn't the Ripper, because his first canonical victim was at the end of August. Yes, there was still speculation about the actual victims, and there was said to be one called Martha Tabram.

I went back to the article and carried on reading about Alfred George Crow, a local cab driver, from the George Yard Buildings, and I guessed I was within walking distance of it. It went on to say that he got home at half-past three on Tuesday morning. He had stated that as he was passing the first-floor landing, he saw someone lying on the ground. Alfred had said that he took no notice because he was accustomed to seeing people walking the streets. In that sense, life hadn't changed. Ed knew that even in his own time, people would walk past individuals in need or trouble. Alfred went on to say that when he got up at half-past nine, the landing was empty. He went on to say that his sleep had not been disturbed by anything.

John Reeves was the next person up to take the stand. Having been to one of these events before, albeit, in my dream, I could imagine the crowded hall and the people bustling to listen to the witnesses and their stories. Mr Reeves again lived in the same buildings and was a waterside labourer. He said that on the same Tuesday morning, he had left home at a quarter to five to find work. When Mr Reeves reached the first-floor landing, there was the victim lying on her back in a pool of blood. He had raised the alarm with a police officer.

I went on to read that woman was not known to live in the area. The police constable was Thomas Barrett; he said that he was alerted to the incident by Mr Reeves. When he discovered that the victim was dead, he sent for a Dr Killeen, who pronounced her officially deceased.

When he took the stand, he went on to tell the jury and coroner that she had 39 stab wounds on her body. He suggested that she had been dead for about three hours. Her age was put at around 36 and healthy for a woman of the area. The doctor went on to record his post-mortem examination findings. It was gruesome, and I wondered, not for the first time, how people could listen to or even read this.

During the examination, the report noted that her left lung had punctures in five places, the right one in two. Her heart – recorded as being rather fatty – had been penetrated once and that would be sufficient to cause death. The liver was healthy which, considering the era, was fantastic, but she had suffered five stab wounds, the spleen had two, and the stomach had been penetrated six times even though it was said to be healthy.

A knife had inflicted the injuries, with the exception of one wound to the chest-bone. The doctor suspected that wound had been inflicted by some kind of dagger and that all of the wounds had happened while she was still alive.

I was intrigued that Jack had used both implements and I wondered why. I always knew a knife as a cutting tool that usually had one cutting edge and was mainly meant for kitchen use. Knives are one of the oldest tools men have ever used. Because of its use in the kitchen, it doesn't need the double cutting edge as found on a dagger. It is a suitable weapon for stabbing as it has a very sharp front and narrow blades at the top that could easily and quickly penetrate human skin.

I knew that Jack carried a cane, and it wasn't uncommon for these innocent-looking items to become a sword or dagger. As to carrying a knife, there was a lot of turbulence, and as I looked around the room, I could only guess how many concealed weapons there were in this room.

The coroner said he hoped that the body could be identified soon. What was not surprising was that three women had recognised Martha under three different names. The case was handed over to the police and adjourned for a fortnight.

13

The strange feeling around me seemed to go against my character. My whole being was disgusted with everything I had seen, felt and read in these dreams, and as the article was making me smile, I questioned again who had me trapped within their body and why?

Why was I happy to read about this horrific murder? I shook my head, trying to clear the fogginess. Looking at the paper, I had this sudden feeling of someone staring at me. So I turned my head to see who it was, but all around me were people shuffling along with their heads down, dressed in drab clothing, trying to dodge the next rain cloud, as well as the horses and carts hurrying up and down the street. Around me was a rank smell of the manure left by the many animals on the roads, as well as the old and decaying horses' manure. I could feel my eyes water with the stench and I could feel it clinging to my lungs with every breath I took. This wasn't a dream. This was real life, and I was somehow in 1888 London again.

Then I realised that I was being watched from within, by the mind that had me trapped, and dare I say a very evil one at that. I didn't know whose it was or how it had happened, but it had. The strange thing was for the first time in these dreams, I could suddenly sense he wanted to communicate. I had felt his reaction as he read this article. There was a very perverse happiness about this poor woman's death. He was smiling inwardly at me, almost laughing at my discomfort.

For the first time, I felt very awake in this street and, looking around, I was surprised at the all the sights and smells around me. You could see the tail end of the market traders and peddlers trudging home with what was left of their day of trading. The rotten fruit and vegetables left in the gutter with rats taking what they could before fleeing a boot. I wasn't unfamiliar with the living conditions of the era. In addition to my past visions and my research I had done on the end of the 19th century, I had studied History at A Level. That said, I was learning faster than Miss Wooster had taught me in school being here and seeing the dire poverty of the East End.

The late Victorian era and Whitechapel were notorious not just for high crime rates, but overcrowded living conditions as well. The homes or slums were overpopulated, with many families being forced to share not more than a room in which they all slept and ate.

With immigration high in the area, they also had to share these places with strangers who could not afford to live anywhere else. These slums were damp and infested with insects and rats. Hygiene was at its lowest because most of the people who lived here shared street water pumps. There was no indoor plumbing as we are so accustomed to nowadays. I remember almost going into meltdown when my flat in my own time had no water, following a burst water pipe. It had meant there was not water for three days and we had to queue in the street by a water tanker waiting for free bottled water. I had felt grubby not showering for just three days. How must these people feel?

I understood that alcohol was a huge part of life in the area, particularly for the poor, and as I looked around, trying to get

CHAPTER 13

my bearings, I saw that we were standing in front of the Ten Bells public house watching the working girls standing on the street corner, teasing the passers-by. I could feel the anger in this strange mind building up.

Then, just as suddenly as the temper was there, he was as calm, and I could feel him smiling. I was assuming this was a man. He had started moving; with the newspaper tucked under his arm and using a cane in his right hand, he strode across the street towards the tavern and doffed his hat to the girls. They jeered at him as he moved towards the pub door.

He pushed the door open, and there in front of me was a mirror behind the bar. I stared at his reflection, wanting to see what body I was inhabiting as he moved towards the gin-soaked woman behind the bar. But the only face I saw in the dirty and tarnished glass was mine. I could feel him within me as he laughed, "This was never going to be easy. Do you think I would let out the secret of my identity that easily?" He hadn't spoken, but I heard his words as if I was standing right next to him. This was not a dream any more, this was real.

"What'll i' be, duck?" the woman behind the bar asked, with a smile that revealed almost no teeth in her mouth and the ones that were there were almost black. "Ale, please, and one for yourself." Her smile broadened, and her chest seemed to have grown. She was a buxom woman to start with, but as his coin hit the beer-soaked counter, her breasts were almost in my face.

I could smell her, too. The smell seemed to arouse him, and I could feel his heart quicken. It was not clear, but I could hear him laugh. "That is why I come here; well that is sort of why. I want to learn what makes them emit that aroma." He laughed at my fear. "Do you want to see me kill her? I can, you know, and if you say yes, she will be dead by sunrise." He started to laugh, again, but this time, it was so loud I thought the whole bar could hear him. Nobody was looking at us.

He picked up the tankard, moved over to the seating around the edge of the place and removed a glove from his pocket to use to move the table out of the way. He set the drink down and the newspaper on the fabric. "What? You expect me to sit in their shit and piss? Do you know, these people are not more than animals with voice boxes? I enjoy watching them, and I am learning so much about them, but I do not want to contract their diseases."

"Why am I here?" I venture to ask.

"That I cannot answer, but you are here, so let us enjoy our time together. My name is ... Oh. That would have been too easy to reveal, but you can call me ... Let us see, you can call me Jack. So, that feels comfortable. Yes, hello, my name is Jack, please to make your acquaintance."

"Ed. Edward Ryder." It felt strange being introduced to this man and you may not believe me, but in my mind we shook hands. That was our first evening together during which we actually talked. Although there wasn't much conversation between us, he seemed more preoccupied with the room in front of us. He appeared to be watching the patrons. It was as if he was waiting for someone.

The strangest sensation was as he sipped his beer; I could taste it, just as I could smell the odours around me, and it wasn't pleasant. In fact, if I had been served that in the bars in my own time I would have sent it back. It was sour, and I swear I saw something floating in it.

After another tankard, he stood up. "I think this is where we part company for a while. I am retiring to my abode, and you

CHAPTER 13

must return to your own world. Until we meet again, I bid you goodnight." And I swear I actually felt him doff his hat to me as I woke up.

As I did, I was pondering how this had happened and realised I was still on the sofa, fully clothed. I had fallen asleep that night, with some music playing. Sandi had gone home early. She had to work early and much as she wanted to stay, her place was closer to work for her.

I sat there pondering the identity of the person in the dream. The man had said his name was Jack, or rather I would know him as Jack, and the only Jack that I know of that age is Jack the Ripper. The blow this hit me with was so strong that I vomited onto my living room floor. Could I have dreamt about him?

As I moved to clean up the mess and myself, I thought back to the stories and history of this unknown assailant of at least five women.

I know some of the stories from the late 1880s. Everybody does. It is part of Britain's infamous folklore. I have read some of the books about the murders of the women in the East End, seen some of the films that were based on the characters. It is one of the most talked and written about stories in history, although it isn't my favourite of stories. I don't like thrillers. I am really a "chick flick" type of person. Sorry, but for a guy, I am a bit of a wimp.

The stories I read and watch have to be happy-ever-after. So how could I have found myself sharing the mind of this weird man and actually sharing in his glee at these poor women's deaths?

Jack the Ripper, the pseudonym given to this Victorian serial killer. He was a man who preyed on some of the most impoverished people in London's East End in the late Victorian era. I remembered that the nickname had come from a letter written at the time by someone claiming to be the murderer. There had been so many suspects put forward, at the time and by historians throughout the 20th century. Everybody coming up with numerous theories, but his real identity and his motives are, even now, still not understood.

I know that in all criminal history, this is the most famous one that remains unsolved. It is arguably about the most notorious serial killer in history and perhaps the most infamous of cult figures. Scarcely the mere mention of his name evokes such fear and imagery. The police at the time and since have tried to unravel the mystery, to solve it. People for years had sought to come up with an answer. Even now, when the last hypothesis was released last year that it was a Polish immigrant, people still disagree, and the famous murders in Whitechapel are still unresolved.

If I was to remember this correctly, there had been five victims that were reported as having been killed with the skilful knife of this unknown assailant, with no clues or leads as to who the person was. Maybe I could discover in my dreams exactly who it was? Maybe I could solve this mystery 125-something years later?

14

Martha's story is so sad, I thought as I researched her short life, but it was so similar to all these poor women of the era in the same situation. On Christmas Day, nearly twenty years earlier, Martha had married Henry Samuel Tabram at Trinity Church in St Mary's Parish, Newington. He was a foreman for a furniture packing company and described as a short but well-dressed man with a grey imperial moustache. They had already been living together but moved to Marshall Street in early 1871.

They had two sons, Frederick John and Charles Henry, but the marriage ended in 1875. It is said that Henry left because of his wife's heavy drinking. When the marriage finally collapsed, she was awarded an allowance of 12 shillings per week to keep herself and her sons. This was reduced considerably because she pestered him for more money in the street when she was penniless, again. As result of this, there was a warrant taken out against him, and he was locked up for non-payment. About the same time, Henry learnt that Martha was living with another man, so he refused to support her after this.

Martha's new partner was one Henry Turner, a carpenter, and they were known to have been living together on and off for around twelve years. In contrast to Henry, he was a short, dirty man who dressed in a very slovenly manner. He was very young-looking with a pale complexion. But he also had an imperial air about him. Their relationship had been significantly affected by Martha's drinking, too. Turner stated at her inquest: "Since she had been living with me, her character for sobriety was not good. If I gave her money, she generally spent it on the drink."

Martha was also renowned for staying out late at night, sometimes not getting back before eleven at night and sometimes staying out all night. The excuses were usually that she had had a violent fit while out and had ended up in one police station or another. Turner had seen her have one or two of these fits and stated at her inquest that they happened mostly when she was drunk.

Shortly before Martha's death, Turner became unemployed and was making his living hawking cheap trinkets, needles and pins as well as menthol cones. They lodged in the house in Star Place, Commercial Road. The landlady Mrs Bousfield had described Martha as someone who would "rather have a glass of ale than a cup of tea". Although she did point out that she was not a perpetual drunk.

About a month before her murder, the couple left their lodgings without giving notice, because of rent arrears. It was thought that, out of guilt or pride, Martha had secretly returned one night and left the key for the landlady, without being seen.

It was around this time that Turner left Martha for one final time.

It was confirmed that he was living at the local home for working men on Commercial Street. Martha had tried to carry on earning a living through selling trinkets and had also turned to prostitution. She spent her small income on drink. This was confirmed by Turner when he was recorded saying: "If I gave her money she generally spent it on drink. In fact, she was always drunk. When she took to the drink, however, I usually left her to her own resources, and I can't answer for her conduct then." It was strange that he contradicted the landlady.

Martha was now living at 19 George Street, Spitalfields, and Turner saw Martha for the last time on Leadenhall Street, near Aldgate Pump, just three days before her death. He said he had given her some money to buy some trinkets to sell on.

On Bank Holiday Monday, Martha went out with Mary Ann Connelly, who was also known as "Pearly Poll". They were seen at different times during the evening in local pubs and in the company of a soldier or possibly a couple of soldiers. According to Pearly Poll, the two women had picked up two guardsmen – a corporal and a private – in the Two Brewers public house, and had visited several pubs, including the White Swan on Whitechapel High Street, and were drinking together most of the evening.

It was close to midnight when Martha and Pearly Poll went their separate ways; Martha with the private and going towards George Yard, and Pearly Poll with the corporal walking into Angel Alley.

Two hours later, Elizabeth Mahoney returned to her home in the George Yard Buildings. As she went up the stairs to her flat, she said at the inquest that she didn't see or feel anything was unusual in the building.

Shortly after this, PC Thomas Barrett saw a young grenadier guardsman in Wentworth Street. This was at the north end of George Yard. The policeman stopped him to question the reason the guardsman was there and was told that he was just waiting for a friend to come back who was with another girl.

An hour-and-a-half later, Alfred Crow returned to his lodgings in the building and noticed what he believed to be someone who was homeless sleeping on the first-floor landing. He shrugged it off as this was quite common and he continued on to his bed.

John Reeves left his lodgings in the building around dawn. By this time there was enough light inside the stairwell. Reeves also saw the body on the landing on the first floor, but he also noticed a pool of blood around the body. He ran off to find a police officer.

When he and PC Barrett returned, although it was not yet identified, they found the body of Martha Tabram. Her body was supine with the arms and hands down by her side. Her fingers were tightly clenched, as if holding something, and the legs were open, suggesting that intercourse had possibly taken place.

The post-mortem examination of Martha Tabram was conducted by Dr Timothy Killeen within an hour of finding her. She was described as a plump, middle-aged woman, about 5' 3" tall, with dark hair and complexion. The time of death was estimated at about three hours before the discovery and examination. There was a total of thirty-nine stab wounds which included five injuries to her left lung and two injuries to her right lung. There was one wound to her heart, five others to her liver, two to the spleen and six to her stomach.

According to the doctor, the focus of the wounds was to the breasts, her belly and groin area. In Dr Killeen's opinion, all the wounds bar one were inflicted by a right-handed assailant, and all but one were the result of an "ordinary pen-knife". However, there was one wound on the sternum which appeared to have been the result of a dagger or bayonet being used.

At the inquest, the saddest part that I read was regarding the clothing. At the time of Martha's death, she was wearing a black bonnet, with a long black jacket over a dark green skirt;

she also had a brown petticoat on, stockings and spring-sided boots that showed considerable age.

In the research that I did for the murder of both Emma and Martha, I came across Annie Millwood, who was the widow of a soldier named Richard Millwood and aged around 38, although her date of birth was not stated on any site I looked at. She lived at Chambers, 8 White's Row, Spitalfields, and like most of these women living in this area may have been supporting herself through prostitution.

On Saturday, 25 February 1888, Annie was admitted to the Whitechapel Workhouse Infirmary. There were reports that she had stab wounds to her legs and lower torso that had been inflicted with a knife. I came across an article in the Eastern Post that seems to shed a little bit of light on the subject:

"It appears the deceased was admitted to the Whitechapel Infirmary suffering from various stabs in the legs and lower part of the body. She stated that she had been attacked by a man whom she did not know and who stabbed her with a clasp knife which he took from his pocket. No one appears to have seen the attack there is only the woman's statement to bear out the allegations of assault, although that she had been stabbed cannot be denied."

As the article reported, she had stated that it was a stranger that harmed her, although all the searching I had carried out to find out more about Annie I could not be sure of the exact number of wounds.

Luckily for Annie, she had made a complete recovery and a month later was released. It looked like she was sent to the South Grove Workhouse, Mile End Road. Sadly, ten days later she collapsed and passed away in the backyard of the building while possibly having sex. The inquest attributed her death to a sudden effusion into the pericardium from the rupture of the left pulmonary artery through ulceration. So, it was natural causes that killed her.

It's interesting, I pondered, that there were many similarities between this attack and the murder of Martha Tabram. Martha's injuries were repeated stab wounds in her lower torso similar to Annie's. Could these two attacks have been at the hands of the same man? I had read that there were proposals that Martha should be included as the "sixth" canonical Ripper victim. Would that mean that Annie was the first attempt? The more I read, the more I questioned things. My main issue was why I was shown these things?

15

Jack the Ripper was never caught, which has added to the mystery. No other killer in British history was known to have rivalled him at the time. He was the most gruesome, mocking, utterly superior figure of Jack the Ripper. A mass murderer whose own arrogance and boldness stumped the entire police force of London and held an entire city in terror and, as I have dreamt, not also did he enjoy this, he encouraged this panic.

The first victim of the canonical five was Mary Ann "Polly" Nichols, who was only 42 at the time of her death. Her body was found on Buck's Row, a secluded area but near to houses and a factory site. She was discovered by a police constable by the name of John Neil, at 3.15 p.m. on 31 August 1888. The Ripper had slashed her throat twice over, and her abdomen had been savagely cut open, exposing the intestines. Her vaginal area had also been mutilated and removed.

She was a short woman at only 5' 2", with brown, greying hair and brown eyes. Her mutilated body was identified by her father, who only recognised her by her missing teeth. It was well known that she had a drinking problem, as did most of the people in the area, and spent the short life she had making ends meet as a prostitute.

Her husband had left her, years before, for another woman. Mary was a mother to five children, the oldest being 21. She was seen as a sad and destitute woman. There had been rumours of her living with a man in the Old Kent Road area, whom she had walked out on before returning to the East End again. It was stated in *The Times* at the time that most people liked her, but also pitied her.

One story about Mary Anne was that she was working as a prostitute and had been drinking on the morning of her death in the Frying Pan Pub, on the corner of Thrawl Street, and was last seen there at 12.30 a.m.

She left the pub probably a bit tipsy.

This would fit with her drinking problems. It was said that she tried to get a bed at the common lodging house located on that road but, having spent the rent money – a mere four pence – on booze, she was turned away. Polly Nichols, as she was known in the area, said that she would go and get the "doss money" which most people believe meant she was going to resort to paid sex to raise the cash. It appears that her confidence was met with some success.

Emily Holland met up with Mary. She was one of the last people to see her alive. This was only an hour before her body was found. They met outside a grocer's shop at the junction of Whitechapel Road and Osborn Street. Emily had stated later that Mary was boasting that she had got the "doss money" and she had earned it "three times over", but had spent it on drink instead. Emily had tried to get her to go back to the lodging house she was staying at and sober up. But Mary announced that she was off to make it one last time. "It won't be long before I'm back."

A carter (I googled this and discovered it was someone who delivered goods, by horse and cart) known as Charles Cross was on his way to work along Buck's Row about an hour later when he passed the gateway that was situated on the left just before the boarding school. He noticed what he thought to be a tarpaulin on the ground. He walked over to investigate it and found that it was the prone figure of a woman with her blood-stained skirts up around her waist.

As he stood there, he was not sure what to do. He looked up at the sound of footsteps behind him. He was greeted by another carter by the name of Robert Paul. They both bent over the body looking for signs of life. Somewhat callously, when they discovered that she was in fact dead, they decided that there was little they could do for her, and carried on to work: they couldn't be late for employment. As they walked away from Mary, they did agree to tell the first policeman they came across.

That was Police Constable Neil, who was walking his regular beat along Buck's Row and who, on getting to Mary, found the woman's throat had been savagely cut back to the spine as he described it. He had shone his light over the woman. Then to get further help he had shone the lantern up and down the Row to grab the attention of PC Thain, who was passing on the far side. When he saw the lamp, he approached Neil and was told to fetch the local doctor, Dr Llewellyn. At about four in the morning, the doctor carried out a passing examination of the woman and seeing the extent of the wounds to the throat, pronounced her dead.

I can say that most of this had happened, just as they had recounted. I had been hiding in the alleyways and watched all of this. I had watched as Mary had walked, or rather staggered, the streets. I had watched her with the men she had picked up and taken to hallways and stairwells for a few moments of privacy. I was shocked that no one had seen me. I didn't understand how a body of a man could hide so well in these streets. I thought that just for a moment I had been seen when Mary had spoken to Emily.

I had not been able to hide so well. I had walked the street, trying to catch the conversation between the two women, and for just a moment I thought he was going to strike both of them. But no. We had gone to the end of the row and waited for Mary to approach. That was it ... I wish I could describe the killing but I can't. I seemed to black out, I am not sure how, but as Mary was knocked to the floor, I saw nothing more until I was walking across the cobbles to this alleyway and hiding, waiting for her to be found.

Jack laughed when he saw the two carters walk off. "Nobody cares for these slags," he said in my head. He was crowing about the two policemen as they struggled to deal with the scene. I knew this was all in my head and that I was the only person to hear his words.

We watched carefully as the doctor moved in more closely to examine the body. I knew from the reports I had read that he had found the body was still quite warm, although her hands and wrists were cold. He had surmised that she had only been dead about half an hour. I knew she had died only twenty minutes before then.

Then luck was on Jack's side, word of the death had begun spreading around the immediate area, and the local workers were arriving to gawk at the crime scene. We moved out of the shadows and joined the crowds as the doctor worried and ordered the two policemen to remove the body to the local mortuary.

We watched as Mary Anne Nichols was placed onto a simple wooden handcart that was used as an ambulance and taken to

CHAPTER 15

the morgue.

16

I sat and looked on as the coroner opened the inquiry into the death of Mary Ann Nichols at the Working Lads' Institute. On the witness stand was Edward Walker and I listened as he spoke. He told the inquest his address and that he was looking for work. He had been a blacksmith. I choked to think of this father looking at the torn body of his daughter in the mortuary and how it must have made him feel. Although it hadn't surprised me to hear him say that he had not seen her for three years. He had gone on to say that he had recognised her by a small mark on her forehead that she had had since she was a child. He also stated that the missing teeth had helped him remember her. Edward had gone on to speak about her marriage to William Nichols and their separation some years before.

The coroner and Edward went on to talk about the letter Mary had sent to her father, about how she was getting on. The letter, which was said to be dated 17 April, was read out to the jury and referred to a place to which Mary had gone in Wandsworth.

When asked when this man had last seen his daughter, with his eyes averted again, Edward told the coroner it had been around two years. Jack was smirking; I hoped no one else noticed his happiness, this was a sombre affair and someone rejoicing in this would not have gone unnoticed.

The next hour was taken up with how Mary had lived her life

CHAPTER 16

and how the father had noticed her drinking and that was one of the reasons they had stopped talking.

Next to speak was the young police constable, John Neil, who stated that he had been proceeding down Buck's Row, in Whitechapel, heading towards Brady Street. The streets were quiet, and he had been down this road about thirty minutes beforehand. Jack smiled inwardly.

Neil had been on the right-hand side of the street when he noticed a figure lying in the street. It was dark at the time, although there was a street lamp shining at the end of the row. He had crossed the road to find the deceased lying in a gateway.

He went on to describe the area, and he said that he examined the body with the aid of his lamp and saw the blood that was oozing from a wound in her throat. PC Neil stated that Mary was lying on her back, with her clothes in disarray. When he touched her arm, it was still warm, and her eyes were wide open. Her bonnet had fallen off and was lying beside her on the left-hand side.

He had seen the other constable passing by on Brady Street and called him over. He told him to run and get Dr Llewellyn, then, seeing another constable on Baker's Row, instructed him to go and fetch the cart they used as an ambulance.

After the doctor had examined the woman, they were asked to move her to the mortuary. The police officers placed her in the ambulance and drove her to the mortuary.

It was there that Inspector Spratley, who had arrived to start taking a description of her, discovered that she was disembowelled. It had been hidden by her clothing. The record stated that a piece of comb and a bit of looking glass were found on her body. She was penniless, but an unmarked white handkerchief was found in her pocket.

JACK

After a lot of backwards and forwards about searches made and what was evident at the scene, the doctor was called to document her injuries. He said he believed her to be a female about 40 to 45 years old, with five teeth missing, and a slight laceration to the tongue. On the right side of her face was a bruise running along the lower part of the jaw. He thought it could have been caused by a blow with the fist or maybe the pressure of a thumb.

On the left side of the face was a circular bruise, which also might have been caused by the use of fingers. On the left aspect of the neck, about an inch below the jaw, there was an incision of about 4 inches long and running from immediately below the ear. An inch below on the same side, and commencing about an inch in front of it, was a circular incision terminating at a point about 3 inches below the right jaw. This incision completely severed the neck down to the vertebrae. These cuts the doctor believed had been caused by a long-bladed knife, that was moderately sharp, and it had been used with some violence.

There was no blood found on the top part of the body or clothes. But there was on the bottom of the abdomen. I wanted to know why there was no blood showing and tried to ask, but I was only a spectator in another mind; even Jack laughed at my question. "Do you really believe she died where they found her? No, I moved her there after the deed was done. I feared I would be seen in the street."

The inquest went on to talk about the 2 or 3-inch wound created in a rough manner. It was a very deep wound, and the tissues cut through. There were also several incisions running across the abdomen. On the right side, another three or four similar cuts ran down the body.

CHAPTER 16

All these had been caused by a knife, which had been used violently and thrust downwards, the doctor said. He believed the cuts were made by a left-handed person and with the same instrument.

The coroner thanked the doctor and because of the late hour adjourned the inquest for the day.

The next victim that was classified within the series of Whitechapel murders was Martha Tabram. She, again and like so many of the women of the time, was a prostitute in the area.

It was said that both Martha and another prostitute were out drinking with two men in soldiers' uniforms, at a public house near the George Yard Buildings. It was shortly before midnight on the Sunday night that the two women paired off with their clients, with Martha heading through the archway into George Yard. Most of the injuries were focused on her throat, chest and lower abdomen. They also appeared to have been inflicted by a small pocket knife, except there was one powerful stab that had gone through her chest. This was believed to have been administered with a large dagger or maybe a bayonet, which led the authorities to believe the soldier she had met was the killer. However, I was still thinking about Annie Millwood when I thought of this murder.

When I asked if he had been responsible for these two crimes, Jack would only answer that Martha's death had been delicious to watch. I was not sure if this meant he was the killer of Martha or not and when I pushed him to commit to them, all he would do was laugh.

I knew he had murdered Mary Ann Nichols and when I had found us walking along Hanbury Road, I knew what was going to happen.

It was in the early hours of the morning of the eighth that I found myself watching someone I assume was Annie Chapman, due to my research on the dates of the murders. She was being turned out of a lodging house because she lacked the few pence needed to pay for the bed. That seemed to be the pattern with these women. Other people were walking about and some were clambering to get past her to take to their beds. Jack was grinning and mumbling her name.

These buildings were like all the others along the street. Overcrowded and, even at this hour, busy with people coming and going. Jack then pulled out his watch fob for me to see the time – it was 5.05 a.m.

As she turned to walk away, I – or rather Jack – followed her, keeping her at a distance. We watched as she staggered along the road. I suddenly realised that she was walking towards the Ten Bells pub, a place I have visited a couple of times before with Jack. This time, we didn't enter. We stood across the way watching the entrance. A man wearing a skull cap walked up to the doors and gingerly opened one. He popped his head inside, and I heard him calling Annie out. With no grace, she exited the pub, and they talked for a moment before moving to the alleyway. I watched as he tried to copulate with her, but the beer had got the better of both of them. It sickened me to watch them as they fumbled with their clothing and as he pushed her against the wall, lifting her skirts.

Annie made an attempt to straighten out her dress and laughed at him and walked towards Hanbury Street, just a short walk from the pub. Her skirts were still in disarray, but the stroll seemed to be helping her. She passed a few workers and other prostitutes, with whom she conversed briefly before entering Hanbury Street.

Both sides of the street were lined with four-storey houses.

CHAPTER 16

Numerous front doors opened into very narrow passageways which led to the staircases for the other floors and on to the backyards. The rooms of these buildings were designed to be let out to individual tenants and their families. A lot of the front doors were left open, for ease of getting in and out of the building I found myself at, Number 29. All the floors seemed somewhat overcrowded, and I watched a few dishevelled people walk around. Most of these tenants work very long hours of the day and night, hence the people milling about, some going into the houses, some coming out.

Jack told me that this was a favourite spot for the prostitutes of the area, and they could be seen taking their clients into the hallways and landings of the buildings or else leading them into the backyards. It had a private feeling about it.

We moved to approach Annie and called out her name. She turned and looked at me and smiled. She greeted me with a very cheery, if not a drunken, slur. As I stood with my back to the street, I watched in the dirty windows a fairly tall and buxom lady walk past. She bobbed her head and called out a morning greeting.

Jack was saying something, I didn't quite catch it, but I heard Annie say yes, as Jack laughed at me.

I woke with sweat pouring off me and turned to Sandi, who was still sleeping.

The clock said it was 5.37 a.m. We had only just gotten into bed about an hour before, so I turned over and waited for sleep to catch me again.

As I lay there waiting, I remember what I had read of Annie Chapman's murder and the man who a witness had seen Annie with just before her murder. That woman had seen me, or rather Jack. Why had they never caught him? Surely the woman had been able to identify Jack? Another witness, Albert Cadosch, who actually lived next door to the murder scene, had reported hearing a woman in the backyard next door repeatedly say "No". This was followed by what he described as a body falling against the fence. It was around twenty minutes later that her badly mutilated remains were found by another carter, John Davis. She was found near a doorway to the backyard of the address.

Again, her injuries were close to those of Polly's. Her throat had been cut in much the same manner; it had been slashed. Her abdomen had been ripped entirely open, with her intestines all torn out but still attached, and placed over her right shoulder. It was in the autopsy that it was revealed that the killer had removed her uterus and some parts of her vagina.

17

We were wandering through the streets again. I knew from the little research I had done and my reading of Charles Dickens at Edinburgh University that the upper and to some extent the middle classes didn't know how the poorest of the poor classes lived. This area of Whitechapel, this wasn't just working class. It was made up of an enormous number of unskilled labourers who were left out of society, almost a forgotten class, who struggled to do menial jobs.

There were no laws to protect these people from safe working conditions and wages. Employment was hard and most sought work in places that could range from making clothes or cigars, to working in sweatshops. I had watched the depressing milieu in which the match workers toiled. I had stood across the way from these young girls, who only looked to be in their teens, going to and from the large factory there. I knew the name, Bryant and May, and I think most people at some point would have struck one of their matches. But these poor girls were going in around dawn and leaving – if they were uninjured – twelve hours later, exhausted.

Then there was the disease that was rampant in the factory. Unlike today there were no separate facilities provided. The girls were expected to eat at their benches, leading to "Phossy jaw", a disfiguring and painful disease.

I knew that the socialist Annie Besant had been so outraged by this exploitation that she had decided to investigate conditions at the plant for herself. It was on 23 June 1888, that after questioning some of the girls at the facility, her shocking exposé in *The Link* was printed. In the article, she had compared the Bow Road factory to that of a "prison-house" and the match girls as "white wage slaves" who were "undersized", "helpless" and "oppressed".

Annie had gone on to state that the girls worked from 6.30 a.m. during the summer and 8 a.m. in winter. They worked until 6 p.m., with only two breaks per day. They were expected to stand all day. Annie wrote that a typical day was that of a young girl, earning around 4 shillings a week. Out of her earnings, 2 shillings was paid for the rent of one room; the children lived on only bread and butter and tea for all their meals.

These salaries were often reduced further by the huge number of fines and deductions bestowed upon them. These fines could be for leaving a match on the work benches. There was also a deduction made for the brushes, paints and other equipment needed to carry out the job.

There was also a high accident rate. The girls were in constant danger of losing a finger or limb or, worse, their health and well-being. Their fingers were often lost to the machinery, and they were not advised to heed this danger because the foreman was not averse to handing out "occasional blows".

The one thing that was sure is that men did make more than women, and this fact made women and children among the poorest in this area. Even if women could find some work in factories or the sweatshops, the wages were not enough to survive on. So, she and her children were reliant on the

CHAPTER 17

breadwinner and the few shillings he could spare her.

It was not uncommon for a woman with youngsters, without a husband, to make a living as a prostitute. Statistics showed that a prostitute was more likely to be roughly mistreated by a "client". That said, generally speaking, crimes against women were rare.

These people, who had to fight to overcome this extreme poverty, were deemed unworthy of the attention of a lot of the social reformers of the time. Yes, there was the first Salvation Army building there, but most of these people were immigrants with poor language skills who for whatever reason had made a home on the streets, hoping for a better life.

Come payday on a Saturday, with their meagre wages, these women could be seen going around the markets and shops clearing their accounts with the baker and the grocers. All in the hope that this would make way for the purchase of meat for Sunday dinner. This was probably the only proper meal they ate each week and, by our standards, the meat would not be fit for consumption, or only close to that.

Whitechapel on a Saturday night was then transformed into streets of stalls. Anything could be bartered for around each of these stalls. There would be women standing about haggling with the salesmen. This could have been for the rancid meat sold there. You could smell it, although I have to say it was hard to separate this from the rotting corpses of the dead horses and faeces all around the streets. The ground was wet and muddy and I was not sure whether it was mud or slurry from the drains. I was just glad I knew I could awaken from this and see the clean streets of Glasgow.

"Glasgow is not that clean," Jack quipped.

"It's cleaner than it was in your time," I replied.

"Tell me about your day. Have you learnt to clear up after the horses?" he asked as he pointed at the bloated body of a mare on the corner of Brick Lane.

This made me laugh. How do I explain to the madman that we use cars? The concept of this was still a decade away, and I didn't believe he would be able to comprehend that. I was then struck by another thought. If I told him about the advancements we had made, did that constitute "changing history?"

"What is funny?"

"Nothing," I answered. "But yes, to answer you, we have found a way to dispose of the dead animals. The streets are crowded, but not with horses."

I was suddenly moved by the sight of a mother trying to replace her son's boots for a pair that didn't look that much better than the ones already on his feet, but at least I heard her say the new ones would keep his feet dry just that bit longer.

We moved on and as the sun was setting I noticed a woman in tears because she had lost half a sovereign. That was every penny her husband had earned that week. It meant she couldn't buy any meat for her family. I, or rather Jack, walked over to her and bent down. He put his hand into the mud, the smell was choking me, but he found a coin and slipped it into her hand. She bent her head in thanks and ran off.

"Why did you do that?" I asked.

"I told you I wanted to understand these people." There was a chuckle. I knew he was lying. "No, to be honest, she didn't deserve the thrashing she would have received at home empty-handed."

We walked on, and I found myself watching the men and women moving in and out of the public houses. They were all

CHAPTER 17

talking in loud voices probably fuelled by the large volumes of beer and gin they were consuming. It was almost as if they wanted their voices to drown all their sorrows.

Some would, no doubt, drink away the hard-earned wages in one night. The women were all poorly clothed, and I knew some would be begging for pennies just to feed their children over the coming week. Some would be selling their bodies, but all of them were selling their souls to survive.

"You are drunk, Mr Edward. I will not abide that in our encounters."

"I am not drunk. I had a couple of drinks, that is all." How did he know this? "You drink, so it is not a crime." Sandi and I had been out the night before and had had a meal with wine. We had moved on to our favourite bar and had a few whiskies, but these people drank more in an hour than I had in one night.

"There is no crime, but I cannot have you jeopardising my life's work. BE GONE."

I woke with a start, with Sandi comforting me. We had both been shocked by the revelation that he knew I had been drinking. I suddenly feared my normal life. If I could enter his time, could he enter mine?

18

In the early hours of 30 September, the Ripper would claim two victims. The first one was Elizabeth Stride. She was discovered in Dutfield's Yard, just off Berner Street, at around 1 a.m. The fatal injury had severed her left artery in her throat, but there were no other slashes or incisions.

Her body was discovered so soon after the wound was inflicted that it was believed the killer had been interrupted, because forty-five minutes later, Catherine Eddowes' body was found in Mitre Square, in the City of London. Again, her throat was severed, and this attack had also involved her abdomen being torn open with a deep, jagged wound. Catherine's left kidney was found to have been removed, along with a major part of her uterus. It was just before the discovery of her mutilated body that an eyewitness saw her with a man who was described as approximately 5' 7" tall, around 30 years of age, and of a medium build. He had a fair complexion and donned a moustache. He had the "appearance of a sailor".

The fear that racked my body at reading this was immeasurable, and every night I went to bed I dreaded waking up in the nightmare. It was a week before I visited Jack again.

"So," Jack said, "you are back, sober, I hope." Yes, I was sober. I hadn't drunk since waking up in Sandi's arms and her telling me about being woken up by me thrashing about in the bed.

CHAPTER 18

Her first thought was that I was having an attack of some sort, but when I had started talking about the woman and the coin, she had waited for me to wake up.

I asked the date in the vain hope that I would miss the "double event".

"Have no fear, Mr Edward; we will not be visiting any deaths tonight. I have people to watch this evening."

With that, we walked off across the road towards the Princess Alice pub, which stood at the corner of Wentworth Street and Commercial Street. I knew that a hundred years later this pub would be remodelled, and renamed the City Darts. Other people were standing around the place, too, but mostly men. The few women out this early in the evening were cheering them on.

I was curious to find out why we were joining this group. The noise from the women was ear-splitting, the cat calls were shrill, and I was confused. "Ah," said Jack, "this is the man I want to see." We turned to see a stout-looking man with short brown to greying hair and a moustache. He was wearing a bowler hat and a black woollen coat.

He looked out of place when compared with the others standing around. He walked to the front of the crowd and took a beer crate from the side of the pub to stand on, and everything hushed.

"Thank you, everybody, for coming here tonight." There was a cheer, and he raised his hands to quieten the crowd. For the next fifteen minutes, he spoke about the good work they were doing and that, for the past fourteen days, they had kept the monster at bay. The women of the area needed to feel safe and able to go about their business knowing that the murderer of Mary Ann Nichols and Annie Chapman had not been able to kill again.

The laughter I felt within me as this man spoke was so loud, I nearly didn't hear the speech. "Oh, you are wrong Mr Lusk," Jack said in my head. "I fear no one."

As the speech finished, we were separated into groups and told where to patrol. We were asked to join George Lusk. He wanted to learn about the new people and the reason they were helping. He spoke to us about his group and how the group of Whitechapel business owners and tradespeople had gathered at the Crown public house.

The group, which possibly included Freemasons, as well as contractors, manufacturers, tailors and others, called themselves the Whitechapel Vigilance Committee, although some preferred the "Mile End Vigilance Committee". They were deeply dissatisfied with the way the police were handling the investigation into all the Whitechapel Murders.

George asked why we were there. Jack was gracious in his replies. He told of how he had read about the group and how it seemed to be working in keeping the streets safe. He spoke of writing a piece for the papers and that he hoped that the man would be apprehended soon.

I suddenly wondered if Jack was a reporter. "No, Mr Edward, it will not be that easy to learn my secrets. These people will believe anything and tomorrow, or the next day, a piece will appear in the papers and Mr Lusk here will think it was me, but the truth is someone is writing about these people."

The whole evening was spent walking the street, carrying lanterns. Checking dark alleyways and questioning and moving men on who seemed to be loitering around. The strange thing was every person we stopped and spoke to was there for a legitimate reason. No one was apprehended for the police to take in, as there had been other nights.

CHAPTER 18

At one point, we had stopped to talk to a sailor and there just up the road was a woman standing under a street lamp watching us. "My sweet Catherine, I hope to see you soon," Jack whispered, almost as if he feared the men around us would hear him. I looked up at her and wanted to shout for her to get out of London.

She was wearing a dark-coloured bonnet, and it was hard to see her features with it in the shadow of the brim, but she seemed to be trying to hear what we were saying. "Be home with you, woman," George shouted at her. "Do you not care that there is a madman on the streets of London?"

She flicked her hand at us and turned to walk away. "You's killing trade, you is," she shouted as she moved off. I wondered if George would ever know that he had met and conversed with a victim?

On the night of her murder, Elizabeth Stride, in what looked like a black jacket and skirt, with a posy of roses and maidenhair fern in her left lapel, with a black crêpe-looking bonnet on her head, was out with a client when I woke up in Jack's mind. She was trying to make the best impression on him. He was a fraction shorter than Elizabeth in height, which was noticeable as they strolled arm in arm. He had a moustache in the characteristic style of the time of the Imperial Age and was wearing a dark morning suit and bowler hat.

It was late, I knew that, but I didn't know what the time was precisely, and we were following the couple. It was strange watching as Elizabeth laughed and giggled at his remarks. She was throwing her head back and lifting her free hand up to her head to cover her mouth. They entered a dark, damp alley. There were puddles everywhere, and the clouds looked like they would open up again, anytime soon. We stood close to the entrance and waited for her to exit alone, with a few coins in her hand.

As she carried on along the streets, we neared Berner Street and hid in a doorway as Elizabeth stopped to converse with a man wearing a peaked cap. We moved out to follow her, but I suddenly felt Jack jump into the door as the police officer walked past us.

As we moved closer to the Working Men's Educational Club, we found her again. This time Elizabeth was in the company of a man who was carrying a long package.

As we stood and watched, two people ran past her shouting at each other. She moved to avoid them, but one was too close to her and with some force pushed her out of the way. She toppled and fell to the ground, straight into one of the many puddles. I watched her pick herself up and brush off the dirt from her skirts and try to wring them dry.

I was surprised she didn't shout out at the men or at least curse, but she just stood there trying to put some dignity back into her appearance.

It was only moments later, after standing around waiting for a lull in the night and arriving at the time when the singing from the hall behind her stopped and the streets were clear, that Jack approached Elizabeth and took her by the hand to the yard entrance. I could feel his excitement growing ...

As I watched the knife glide against her neck, there was a spray of red that hit Jack's face. I almost blinked my eyes to stop the blood getting there. She was on the ground with her eyes looking up, with fear like I have never seen before.

There was a silent scream that seemed to be stuck on her lips. Her complexion had turned from a rosy one to white, and as the life drained from her body, she went limp. Then the smell

CHAPTER 18

hit me; I could almost taste the coppery smell.

Suddenly, there was the sound of a horse cart entering the yard. It was still dark, and there was no light behind us, causing Jack to stop, placing the still damp knife in his pocket. He stood up and waited for just a moment, before realising that the cart was entering the yard. There was a horse just inches from me.

Suddenly the horse jerked upwards; its front legs brushing Jack's face. He moved very fast; I felt us leap to the side as the horse shied high in front of us, before coming back to the ground. We landed up against the wall that enclosed the yard, with a thud. The air was knocked out of us. The last thing I remembered was his body hitting a cold, damp wall before waking up. It woke me with a shock. I had realised that sound had scared Jack, and that was a new sensation.

I lay there for a moment or two trying to catch my breath. I felt winded, and my back was sore. I moved my arm back to see if it was wet and was relieved to feel just my dry skin. I raised my hand to my face, expecting to feel blood on my cheek, but again it was dry. I got up and went to the bathroom, turning on the light and squinting in the glare, waiting for my eyes to adjust. Once they had, I checked my face and, using the shaving mirror, looked for signs of bruising. The relief I felt was immense because I had doubted my sanity.

I had decided that these visions were stronger and more intense than just dreams, so I had made an appointment to see my doctor to talk about this and to see if maybe I could talk to someone.

After rinsing my face, drinking a glass of water and relieving myself, I went through to the living room and picked up the laptop, taking it through to the bedroom. Sitting back in bed, I opened the story of Elizabeth Stride. I needed to read the account of this murder and discovered that close to one in the morning, Louis Diemschutz, a steward of the Workers' Club, had driven into the yard with a pony and two-wheeled cart. His horse had shied as he had entered, and the yard was so dark that he was unable to see anything let alone a body.

When he had come across the body, there was blood still flowing from a wound in her neck; she had only just died.

19

I was sitting in the doctor's waiting room, glancing up at the board looking to see my name coming up. I decided that I would read the account of Elizabeth's death. I was shocked that Jack had been that close to being caught.

In the hour before Louis had entered the yard, there had been people leaving the hall that adjoined the backyard. They had been attending a debate on "The Necessity of Socialism Among Jews", which was followed by a short period of community singing. All those that had been questioned had said that they had seen nothing unusual happening in the yard. Even a woman who lived close by had reported that she had been listening to the singing at about the same time but hadn't seen anyone enter the yard. Mrs Mortimer did report seeing a man with a shiny black bag race past Elizabeth. This had caused a media frenzy with the press speculating on whether this was the Ripper, that was until he had been identified as Leon Goldstein and, after being questioned by the police in charge of the inquiry, had been eliminated as a suspect.

The police had searched all the members of the club and all the adjacent properties. They had interviewed all the residents in the area and had found a witness named Israel Schwartz who had reported seeing Liz, as she was known, being attacked and thrown to the ground outside Dutfield's Yard shortly before she was found.

Israel had said that the attacker had called out "Lipski" to another man walking nearby, but unfortunately, Israel didn't testify at the inquest. The papers speculated that the reason for this was that possibly he was Hungarian and spoke very little if any English. There was another witness, James Brown, that said that around the same time, Elizabeth or someone matching her description had been seen rejecting the advances of a stoutish man who was slightly taller than her. This was said to have happened on the adjacent street to Berner Street. Most of this fitted what I had seen.

Louis later testified that he believed that someone was still in the yard when he drove in. But I knew that he never saw Jack. Louis said that his first reaction was to check that his wife was okay, before going back to the body and raising the alarm. I wondered what Jack had done, how had he got out of there? Had it been when Louis had gone into his home? I was scared to sleep and ask. I needed to get help.

Just as I started to read more, I saw my name come up on the board and stood to walk to the doctor's room. My legs suddenly give way, and I grabbed the back of the chair to try to steady myself. That was the last I remember before waking up lying on the bench in the doctor's room, and she had me hooked up to the blood pressure monitor with a white clip on my finger.

"How are you feeling, Mr Ryder?" Dr McKenzie asked. "You gave the room out there a bit of a scare. I am wondering if you need to go to the infirmary." She had a very soft Scottish accent, and I knew she was from Edinburgh.

"No," I answered. "I am okay. I am just not sleeping well. I don't take those tablets all the time, so I am still having the dreams we spoke of before."

CHAPTER 19

Dr McKenzie checked the results of the machines attached to me, and after jotting down her findings, turned to me and said, "Your blood pressure is a bit high, and your pulse is fast, but nothing to worry about. I know from the receptionist that you didn't hit your head so, okay, let's get you up, and you can tell me what is going on."

I sat up, and after the initial wooziness had passed, I swung my legs off the bed and went to get down to move to the chairs. Dr McKenzie put her arm out and told me to stay. "That fall was hard, and I don't want you moving for a while." With that there was a tap at the door and I watched the doctor go to open it. There was a softly whispered conversation, and after about a minute the door was closed, and Dr McKenzie was standing in front of me again. "Okay, my last two patients are going to be seen by Dr Grant, so you have my attention."

I started trying to gather my thoughts and how to ask for help, but Dr McKenzie made it easy. She first asked if the dreams were still happening and how often. We sat there together going over everything. I was candid in explaining the visions and didn't find it hard to explain the fear. Dr McKenzie was easy to talk to, and I opened up completely.

"Okay," she said a while later, "let's cover the basics. Is the smoking still the same?" I nodded my head. "Drinking?"

"I haven't drunk anything for about four days. I know that sounds bad but, as I have told you, I am not a big drinker. I just like the occasional drink." She nodded her head and made a few notes.

We covered my eating habits, and all the other standard questions doctors ask. "I think you do need to go and see a specialist. What I can't figure out is which one." She went over to her large wooden desk and tapped something into her computer. "To my thinking, I think we need to get a CT scan done. Maybe even an MRI. Now, with those tests, I believe that you may need to see a neurologist." She must have seen my face. "Don't worry, it is only to get them to help read the results."

She then told me that, depending on the results, maybe a sleep clinic would help. But she thought that it might help, in the meantime, to speak to a psychologist. "I have a good contact in this field. I will talk to him today and see if I can get you an appointment in the next day or two."

20

"Ed, what is this all about?" Sandi sat there in front of her boyfriend with his laptop on the table. She had just read his first draft of the book he had spent the last five days writing.

"Sorry, I didn't want to scare you. Yes, I went to the doctor and no that bit about me collapsing didn't happen, well …" He looked at her face and knew he wasn't going to get away with not telling her "… it wasn't that big a deal. Yes, I did have a turn when I stood up and collapsed on the floor, and yes, the doctor is sending me for tests." Ed smiled at her. "I have the MRI being booked. It is classed as urgent but could still take a week or so to come through. The CT scan will only happen if the MRI shows something sinister."

He picked up his coffee cup and took a sip of the near cold liquid; he stood to refill both their cups. "I am going to see the psychologist, just to check that I am sane," he said with a bit of a giggle; even he thought that was inconclusive with everything that was going on. He had meant to tell Sandi about the collapse in the doctor's waiting room the night before when she had come around after work, but Ed didn't want to see the look on her that he saw now.

It had not been as bad as he had written, it had been worse. He had worried about the surgery, but when Ed had explained that he hadn't eaten that day and it was three in the afternoon, the doctor had said that could be a factor. But she was arranging for the test to rule out anything nasty. He was given a biscuit to eat and a cup of tea. It had helped. He had been told that the only factor that had kept him out of the hospital was that Ed had improved with the nourishment and because he had agreed to the tests as well as to take the medication regularly till the results were in.

Dr McKenzie had suggested that he go home and rest, after making the appointment with the radiology department at the Royal Infirmary. She had told him that she would arrange the other appointments and he should hear back from the said units within a day or two.

But he had arranged to meet Sandi when she finished work at five that evening. He had broken his date for lunch twice before, telling her that he had decided to write his first draft of the book, and they had decided that rather than break his concentration that she would come around to his place.

They had decided to meet up and have a quick bite to eat in town. Ed had gone out feeling ravenous until the food appeared. They were at a local steakhouse, and each ordered a large rare rump steak. However, as he cut into it, all he saw was Elizabeth Stride lying before him. He made the excuse that he was tired and his hunger wasn't as great as he thought. Sandi had worried about him, as he was looking a bit peaky.

The two had left the town in the early evening and had headed back to his flat. Sandi had quickly rushed round and tidied it up, knowing that he would have neglected it over the past few days. But she had been shocked to see that he had done most of the basics. Ed had even changed the sheets. He didn't let her know that having woken up in the early hours of that morning, he had been that unnerved that cleaning the flat had helped to

CHAPTER 20

take his mind off the murder of Elizabeth Stride.

While she walked through the apartment and then into the kitchen to make some coffee, he quickly wrote up the chapter with Dr McKenzie and, after a quick spell check, presented it to Sandi to read, who was now sitting in the armchair ready to read it.

He smoked four cigarettes while she read his book draft, realising that he was almost chain-smoking. He was suddenly very nervous about her reaction. "So?" he asked as she finished and looked up at him standing at the window.

"Do you have any idea how good this is? I know it needs work, but not a lot," she said.

"No, it's not polished enough yet. I need to do more work on it," he said. "I think I need an editor to look at it. I mean I wrote this in less than a week, and I am not sure if it sits right."

"Stop doubting yourself. I like it."

Ed stubbed out his latest cigarette and laughed. "You are biased." He moved over to the chair and sat on the arm beside her. "I will say I am scared, really scared. Last night was the closest I have come to seeing a murder. I mean I can still smell the blood that hit me when that knife went through her skin. I haven't put that in that chapter. Yes, mainly because I wrote that quickly this morning and I hadn't had a chance to think about it."

Ed took a large gulp of the coffee in front of him. "I only have two murders to go. Well, I hope I do. But what if he did kill the other women, the unattributed ones? Am I going to experience all their deaths?"

"To me, Jack seems to be enjoying my watching it all. I guess I could say he likes the audience, which in a sense makes it weird that he never got caught. I know from the research I have done into serial killers that they thrive on the public attention. Yes, I know I have been there with him at the courts or stood there as he watched the aftermath of his work. I wonder if it was police incompetence that led to them failing, or did they know who it was and have to hush it up, due to the scandal it would cause?" Ed moved back to the window. "I need to get away from it for a few days."

Sandi stood and walked towards him and held him tight. "You need a drink." Ed shook his head. "Yes, you need to sleep without him in there." She stood up and went to the kitchen, coming back a short while later with two enormous whiskies.

Ed took the glass from her, hoping that it would stop any dreams that night, what with this and the tablet.

21

Ed and Sandi woke the next morning with very thick heads. They had downed three of the whisky measures and, when sleep had started to creep in, they had moved into the bedroom. There had been a fumbled attempt at lovemaking, but both were very tipsy and tired, so they curled up in each other's arms and fell asleep.

Ed had been pleased to wake up refreshed and free of the visions. It had been a pleasure to wake up without the images of dead women. They got out of bed, and after they had both visited the toilet, Ed grabbed Sandi and pulled her into the shower with him.

They were in the kitchen a little while later, drinking their first coffees of the day, wrapped in white bathrobes. They were wondering whether to go out and eat or should they cook at home. Going out won and Ed moved over to the sink to have his morning smoke. He lifted the blind to open the window, and a wall of freezing wind hit him.

"It's snowing," he said, not that he was shocked. He turned to see Sandi reading his book again.

"You're right. We need to get an editor to read this, or at least someone who knows about writing. Could one of your lecturers look it over?"

Ed thought about it for a moment and agreed that he could

contact Sam Petersen, his professor, who had said that he was willing to look at anything the students wanted him to. He pulled out his phone and scrolled for Sam's number. When he called the number, it went through to his voicemail, so Ed left him a brief message and his number.

The pair finished their coffees and went into the bedroom to dress. They both dressed warmly, which in the centrally heated flat was suffocating but, having put on their boots and coats, gloves and hats, they walked down to the street.

Both of them were hungry and waited impatiently for the bus, along with other residents of the area. Everybody was shifting on their feet, trying to keep the warmth in, and when the bus came, everybody let the elder passengers on first, before getting on, bustling for the back seats where the fan heater was.

It was only a short journey to the centre and, after alighting the bus close to Sandi's flat, they hurried to their favourite café near George Square. The reason this was one of their favourite haunts was that the outside area had gas heaters, for the smokers. They took their favourite seat in the corner. It was covered by two of the heaters, so was always cosier.

Taking a menu each from the nearly frozen waiter, just dressed in a shirt and bow tie with a grey-and-white apron tied around his waist and trousers, they pretended to read it, both knowing what they were going to order. They ordered the classic burger for Ed and the Brie and mushroom burger for Sandi. They also ordered a tomato and basil salad with some chips to share.

Ed lit up a Regal as they waited for their coffees to arrive and noticed Weegie walking towards them. He smiled and waved Weegie over. Sandi commented that the figure walking their way didn't look happy, despite the smile. As Weegie sat down,

CHAPTER 21

it was indeed very apparent that Weegie was unhappy about something. Once he was comfortable and there was a cup of coffee in front of him, Weegie slowly rolled a cigarette and lit it before eventually speaking.

"She's deed," he said eventually. Both Sandi and Ed looked at each other with puzzled looks on their faces. "Fiona," he said, but seeing that neither seemed to know who he meant, he went on to tell them that he had received a letter from his solicitor that his wife had died the week before. He explained that when he had left his old life, Weegie had made provision that he was kept abreast of the well-being of his family. He may have left them many years before, but it didn't stop him caring for and loving them.

After his release from the hospital, when he had last seen Fiona, he contacted the solicitor he had used for years before and had asked if they would work on his behalf, but the family were to never know about this. He did suspect that Fiona was aware of this agreement, as when she was asked if she wanted to declare Weegie dead seven years after his disappearance, Fiona had refused, saying that she believed he was out there watching them and while that was so he would stay alive and married to her.

Weegie was shocked that she never dated anyone after he left and that Fiona spent her time helping in local shelters. She never ventured into Glasgow, and Weegie believed that was out of fear of seeing him again, not because she didn't want to see him, but because she did want to see him. Fiona kept herself busy bringing up her three children, watching them get married and delighting in becoming a grandparent.

Weegie had ventured out to the little village where they all still lived and was hidden behind the gravestones in the local church as his eldest daughter, and her husband came out holding a baby in her arms all clad in white. He had recognised the shawl around the baby as the one that had been handed down the family line and had been used at his children's christenings as well as his own. He had seen the smile on Fiona's face as she exited the church and was handed the baby for photos. Weegie had to admit she was still a stunningly beautiful woman and for a moment wondered what was keeping him away from her.

But he knew that Fiona didn't need him back in her life. They were different people and, yes, although he was aware that he was still in love with her, he also knew that to be indoors would not be good for him. The freedom he had had for the past thirty years had been his salvation.

It was hard to think that Fiona was only 64 and now dead. She had been out with friends one night the week before when a drunk driver had hit her, killing her instantly. Weegie had tears in his eyes and was trying his hardest to stop them rolling down his face. He wanted to be with his children, but he knew that was not the best solution.

"Do you think the solicitor can help?" Sandi asked as the waiter walked out with their food and set it in front of them all. "Can we get you anything?" she asked suddenly, realising that Weegie hadn't ordered anything.

Weegie shook his head. "Na, cheers, I'm okay." He turned his chair and rolled another cigarette; he went to light it and realised that Ed and Sandi were eating.

Sandi nodded her head, to give her assent to his smoking. He shook his head and placed the roll up down on the table and picked his cup up. "Ah hud wondered aboot seeing if ah cuid send a letter tae th' bairns juist tae let thaim ken that ah aye care, bit I'm nae sure it wid be richt. Ah jalouse Fiona ne'er let thaim think o' me as deid, sae in thair hearts thay ken a'm alive." His accent was stronger than normal, and both Ed and Sandi had to listen carefully to him to understand him. "Th' funeral is th' morra, 'n' a'm aff tae be thare, in th' shadows. Ah can't be seen, yit."

"We would like to take you if you let us," Ed muttered in between mouthfuls of the burger; he was anxious to eat it while it was hot but didn't want to seem rude to Weegie. "We can hire a car and drive over to the coast. It will be good to get away from the city and my story for a day."

The tears rolled down Weegie's face, and he used the sleeve of his coat to wipe them away. Never before had two people shown him such generosity. So, while they sat there and ate the food and drank the coffee, and Weegie helped them with some of the chips, they made plans.

22

Weegie walked up to the front door of the home he had not set foot in for three decades, and tapped lightly on the wood, almost as if he wanted to stay unheard.

We had talked about it the day before and to Mr Hughes, his solicitor, who had said that he would inform the family that Weegie wanted to see them and ask if they would allow him to attend the funeral. It had impressed us all that the children had said yes and that they looked forward to seeing their father the next day.

We were shocked to see the door open and see Sarah, his eldest daughter, standing smiling at Weegie. She pulled her father towards her and embraced him. "Mother always said you would come back. And we knew you were out there somewhere." she said into his collar with tears in her eyes as she took Sandi and me in.

"Ah, the image of Catherine," said a familiar voice behind me. I turned sharply to see who it was. I had hoped to see someone I knew, but all there was were a few strangers getting out of their cars that they had parked in front of the house and that was some distance from where I stood. The voice had seemed closer, and it was a voice I knew. I surveyed the people, and it was obvious that no one appeared to be looking at me or the door and all were strangers to me. Some were gathering up

CHAPTER 22

flowers and cards and just talking among themselves.

Then there was that laugh, a sound I knew well. I shivered and turned to face the door to see Sandi, walking into the house followed by Weegie and his daughter. I was hoping that I was wrong about the voice, but I couldn't be sure.

The hall was brightly light, and there were photo frames on the sideboard under the stairs. I stopped to look at them all and saw Weegie as he had been on his wedding day. The smiles on his and Fiona's faces were a joy to see. There were photographs of him with each of his children in christening gowns and lots of images of the family as they grew up. But when I looked at the pictures carefully they seemed to stop when the child, that I took to be Sarah, was about 6, maybe 7 years old. That must have been when Weegie disappeared.

The others had made their way into the sitting room, and I rushed to join them. It was a larger room than I expected and seemed to have been divided into two sections; at one end, it was furnished with two oversized sofas either end of the width with two armchairs being used to form a box. There was a huge coffee table in the middle that was covered in condolence cards. At the other end, one oversized sofa, two armchairs and four carver chairs in an irregular semi-circle faced a wall of bookcases, crammed full of novels.

I walked over and glanced at some of the titles. I wasn't shocked to see writers such as Stephen King and James Herbert. These books were always favourites with older women. There were also newer writers there such as Adam Croft and Stephen Edgar. I was very familiar with these authors. I scanned the shelves and was pleased to see some of the classics there, such as Christopher Marlowe, Ben Jonson, Jane Austin and Virginia Woolf.

As I was taking some of the titles, I suddenly heard someone talk to me. "What colourful covers, and some so graphic, but where is Charles, or Shakespeare?" I turned to see who it was that had spoken, but I wasn't surprised to see I was alone. I realised that the worst had happened: Jack was in my world, and he didn't seem shocked at the sight of cars or the fashions. He was admiring the room the same way I had, and if anything, he appeared to be at home. I realised that Jack had been in my mind in my time for some time now. Only he knew how to live in the shadows and watch.

"Why are you here, Jack?" I asked him.

"Oh, Mr Edward, you always had such great images in your head when you joined me; and I was intrigued. I so wanted to see your world; I wanted to experience it the same way as you had seen mine. I have to say one thing; you do have cleaner streets. There is no rotting corpses and shit to avoid. That must be a good thing as these metal things you use to get you around would be destroyed in my world. I want to understand you better; I want to learn. Would you be willing to educate me?"

I answered him rather tersely, saying no. I went on to explain that he could never really understand my world, he wasn't part of it, Jack would never fit in and, after a short argument, he conceded, although I got the impression it was just a ruse.

I realised now that he seemed more intrigued by Sarah and her two sisters. "My, my. I must say that it is like looking at Catherine thrice. You never met her. I lost you so abruptly in the yard. I thought I was going to be caught for sure. But luck was on my side."

I was looking around the room hoping to lose the images Jack was playing in my head, and I tried to concentrate on watching

CHAPTER 22

Weegie being greeted by his family. Sandi was by his side and shaking the hands of the children. She looked back at me and looked worried just for the moment, but I smiled at her and turned to take a book from the shelves. She turned back to the conversation.

I looked down at the book I had selected and it was Patricia Cornwell's *Portrait of a Killer*; as it opened in my hand, and as I started scanning the pages, Jack was laughing. I realised that my nose was running, so I lifted my hand up to rub it away.

I was shocked to see as I looked down at my hand as it moved away from my nose that there was a smear of blood on it. I suddenly felt Sandi take my other hand and the book away from me and ask if I was okay while giving me a tissue she had up her sleeve.

I told her I was, and that it must be the toll of the last few weeks that was catching up with me, that I was just tired. I wiped the blood away and, holding the tissue, pinched my nose to stop the bleeding. We had turned away from the room in the hope of not attracting attention.

I asked if it had stopped and Sandi nodded, before leading me over to the reunion. I briefly spoke to Sarah, Beth, Ruth and Kenny. I also met their partners and three children, and for the next thirty minutes, as we waited for the cars to arrive, I blocked out Jack and enjoyed the conversation that the young adults and children were having with their father and grandfather. I had learnt in that short time that Weegie's name was George, but to me he was Weegie, and I hoped I could still call him that.

The day before, we had spent an hour or so buying him a new suit and taking him to the hairdressers, and I had to admit the new look suited him; it had been strange to see the discomfort in Weegie as the salesman measured him. It had taken all our powers of persuasion to allow the young girl to wash his hair before being trimmed by the stylist. It had not occurred to us that this was new to Weegie.

Because we had wanted to make an early start, we had insisted that Weegie stay in my spare room. He had reluctantly agreed, but the flat was frozen most of the night as Weegie couldn't cope with the heating. "You are too soft on this man, Mr Edward," Jack was saying. But I hoped to win the fight, and when I ordered Jack to leave. I felt relieved when he seemed to disappear.

It was only later in the church, and amongst the mumbled voices from the congregation as the coffin was carried in by six men from the funeral home, that I realised that Jack was still there, albeit in the shadows. But I sensed him lurking there and taking everything in, educating himself.

The sound of Bach echoed around the building as we stood at the front of the church surrounded by Weegie's children. The service began, and those around me knelt in a front pew. However, I wasn't that religious, so felt it better just to bow my head.

"Ah, you be an agnostic, then?" Jack said. I tried to blot him out again.

So began the funeral of Fiona McDonnell, the beloved wife of George and devoted mother of Sarah, Beth, Ruth and Kenny. I learnt that her grandchildren were called George, Fiona and Catherine. She had led a very busy life helping people in crisis and was a strong voice in the mental health sector. It had not shocked me to hear that she had never given up on her marriage and she had understood why Weegie had disappeared.

The vicar told the congregation about the visit to the hospital shortly after Weegie had gone. She had told friends and family

CHAPTER 22

that she had seen him in the bed and at that moment she had known he was happier than she had seen him in years. She had always hoped that he would just come home when he was ready. I turned to see Weegie crying, with two of his daughters holding his hands.

"She'd have liked her funeral," a friend observed outside the church as we stood greeting the people coming out.

"Aye, ah think she wid hae," he answered. Weegie turned to Sandi and me, his eyes red. "Kin we gang soon?" he asked me.

"Are you sure?" And seeing him nod I knew he needed to be back in his comfort zone. "Okay, but you must say goodbye to your children."

I stood there and watched him go up to each of his children and grandchildren, spending time with each one.

"Can I have your number, please?" Sarah asked me, having spoken to her father.

I got out my phone and sent a text to the number she gave me. She said that all of them understood that their father's home was on the streets, but now that they had reconnected with him they wanted to stay in contact. We both smiled and understood completely. We promised that when we were with him, we would get him to phone her.

We left Seamill, with a very subdued Weegie.

23

"Now, Mr Edward, you will listen to me," said a very stern voice from inside my mind. Jack was almost angry. I had spent most of the day before and the morning trying to block him out. I had taken one of my tablets the night before in the hope of getting some sleep, but my headache was back.

It was now evening, and I was sitting in the flat; Sandi had gone home earlier in the afternoon as she needed to be up early the next morning for work. We had got home the day before and dropped Weegie off at the shelter as he had asked. He told me that he was going to get the clothes back to me, I told him to use them to get some food and tobacco. Weegie had smiled sadly and shown us the wad of twenty-pound notes he had in his pocket.

"Mah bairns," he responded. "Thay ken mah need tae bade oan th' streets, bit thay hae tellt me that thare is dosh tae keep me alive. Ah think this wid keep th' hail shelter alive."

I smiled at him and told him to be careful. When we were back at my flat, I told Sandi about the encounter with Jack. She looked shocked and told me I should chase up the appointments, which we had done already earlier that day; I had the psychologist booked for the following week, as to the MRI I was told to phone the next day.

However, my biggest problem at this moment was Jack was

CHAPTER 23

back and I was alone with this madman.

"Please go. It is not your time, you shouldn't be here," I said, picking up my cigarettes and lighter. "I don't understand why you are here."

"Ah, I am not sure either. But as we know this is happening for a reason and we now have the evening to discuss it. There is something I would like to confabulate, and that is Catherine. It was intriguing seeing those three Catherine facsimiles, It has made me curious, I would like to see more of these women in your time. Sandi is quite stunning. She is a good companion to have at this moment. Now, before we continue, I think I need to tell you about the one I 'murdered', that you missed, I believe that you would have enjoyed that."

He went on to tell me that after the interrupted death of Elizabeth, he had managed to get out of the yard when the "idiot", as he called Louis, went into his house. Jack was enraged that he had not had the opportunity to mutilate the body and to show me his technique. I told him that this killing was sickening to me. He laughed and said that everybody was capable of killing. I couldn't agree with him.

Jack went on to say that when he got out of the yard, he moved quickly, searching for something to help take away the anger that was raging within himself, and ended up in Mitre Court and there was Catherine. But as he went to approach her he caught sight of a police officer walking towards him. Jack had stepped into a doorway and waited. Thankfully for Jack, the square was quiet, and he was able to apprehend Catherine quickly and quietly.

"I left her on her back, and her head turned. I decided to give the police a graphic show. The idiot at that yard had spoilt my evening, so I was going to have fun with Catherine. I was nearly interrupted with her by a flat foot, but he turned away from Catherine and I as he passed.

"I placed her arms by her side and her palms upwards, the fingers bent slightly. I left her stomach exposed. And her right leg was bent.

"First, I needed her subdued, it had to be faster than the others as I knew the police would be alerted to Elizabeth very soon. My luck, this time was holding, Catherine was easy to locate, thought I had to depose of her quickly, I went for her face, first. The knife across the throat did not give me the same thrill as before. But I still found pleasure in gutting her."

I had read Catherine's autopsy and had been shocked at the amount of violence Jack had inflicted. They had described the injuries to the intestines, how they had been drawn out and placed over the right shoulder. There had also been a piece of about 2 feet that had been detached from the body and placed between Catherine's body and her left arm. And here was the man himself delighting in explaining it all to me.

I remembered how the report had described how the face had been subjected to cuts up to a quarter of an inch through the lower left eyelid. How the upper eyelid was scratched, and the other eyelid was cut through to about half an inch.

There was a deep cut over the bridge of the nose that extended from the left side down to the jaw and then up the right side. Catherine's nose had been detached and a cut divided the upper lip from the gum and her incisor tooth.

"And," he concluded, "after looking at her liver and removing some to put on display, I thought I would take the kidney, just for the fun of it. I wanted to see how good Abberline was."

He laughed at this. "Did you know that they believe I sent it to Lusk and wrote him a letter? Well if they think I would do

CHAPTER 23

something so idiotic they will never catch me.

"Have you heard the latest idea to apprehend me and that is with a dog?" He gawped. "A dog I ask you." He seemed to be growing more agitated in my mind. "I was at the Royal Parks yesterday and watched as that idiot Charles Warren, whom I gather had contacted a breeder of bloodhounds, used two dogs to find men hiding somewhere in the park. It was hilarious to watch. I mean people hiding from dogs." He stopped talking for a moment and seemed to be listening. "I am unsure if I will be able to continue if they are used. They did appear to be effective on the day."

Jack went on to talk about Edwin Brough, a famous dog breeder of the time who had been approached to help track the killer. Brough had misgivings about using his dogs and was not sure how they would behave in a crowded city environment, but he brought two of his best dogs to London to test their capabilities to follow the scent of a man. If the experiment worked, it was said that Sir Charles planned to buy the dogs. The two bloodhounds in question were 4-year-old Barnaby and Burgho, who was 2 years old.

The dogs were taken to Regent's Park in London to perform the first of several trials. Barnaby and Burgho successfully tracked a young man, even with his fifteen-minute start, and the dogs followed the man for nearly a mile over the frost-covered ground. That evening they were taken to Hyde Park for a further test. This time on the leash because this is how they would have been used in the pursuit of Jack. Again, it was a success even in the dark. The following day, there were a further six separate runs made, in two of which Sir Charles acted the part of the wanted man.

Every time, Barnaby and Burgho captured the person who

was being hunted. Everyone seemed pleased with the results of the trials, but Sir Charles wanted more experiments to be carried out before making the final decision. There was also talk that Sir Charles himself had said the trials had failed on the second day and this was why they were not used.

Then, to hamper the whole thing, critics started mocking Sir Charles over this venture. Some experts in the police force felt dogs were unsuitable for this type of job and that the dogs may inadvertently cause an innocent man to be caught and accused of the crimes. By the end of October, the police had not bought the dogs, or given the assurance they would. So Brough took Burgho to a dog show and never returned him. He eventually took Barnaby back from his London handler, too.

I knew from my research that within days, another brutal murder occurred and some wonder if the killer would have been brought to justice if the dogs had been used.

It was in an interview some years later that Brough mentioned: "Our experiments in London showed that the hounds will hunt a man who is a complete stranger to them, although the line may be crossed by several other people. They were not put to the test so far as the Whitechapel murders were concerned, for no murder was committed during the time the hounds were in London. This I consider some evidence of the deterrent effect which the employment of bloodhounds would have on crime, for another of the ghastly Jack the Ripper tragedies was committed shortly after it was known that the hounds had been sent back to Wyndyate." I had been amazed to have found this story, thanks to Sandi's timeline, and seeing the mention of the testing of bloodhounds in London I had decided to see what had happened and why they had not been used.

CHAPTER 23

I had never heard of this before reading of it and hearing Jack talk about it. To my mind, this could have caught Jack. Today they are used in airports and the like to track drugs and contraband as well as people. So why did they not use them?

"What are airports, Mr Edward?"

"Get out of my head."

24

Now Ed was scared. He hadn't dreamt of being in Victorian London for nearly ten days, but Jack was with him in 2016 every day, and almost every waking hour. He found he was struggling to deal with normal daily chores.

Ed was still writing, transcribing the events and researching the history of the Ripper. But it was harder. The story he thought he was going to write was now more about the research he was doing. Jack wasn't developing things to help him.

When his old professor, Sam Petersen, called him back to say that he would gladly look at his work and assess the merits of publishing it, Ed hesitated. He wasn't sure that it was ready to be read by anyone, but Sandi convinced him that it was the right thing to do, that it would let them know whether he had something. So, they printed off the story that Ed had completed and sent it to Sam.

Ed's biggest problem was Jack and his intrusion in his life. It was like a constant headache, one that wouldn't go; he had tried to ignore the constant questions and observations, but this seemed to anger Jack, and he would shout until Ed responded.

Sandi had noticed that Ed was taking both Nurofen and paracetamol at an alarming rate and had questioned him about it. Ed hadn't been aware of this and had agreed to see the doctor about it.

CHAPTER 24

"Your pubs do not smell. There is no aroma on the streets other than food," Jack said when Ed had decided to meet up with Sandi after work and had gone to a pub for dinner. As was the norm, they were sat outside, and Jack had asked why they didn't sit inside, saying it was surely warmer and there was no snow falling on them.

Ed had explained the smoking laws and that because he was a smoker, he was obliged to sit outside. It was better than having to get up to have one. Ed was struggling to have a conversation with Sandi, and moved his hand towards hers and squeezed it. It was like an unwritten signal between them. She smiled at him, again worried.

To her in the past few days, Ed had deteriorated, and he was wearing dark glasses; he had told her that it helped him, but he couldn't explain why. She knew he heard voices and knew that tomorrow they should have answers.

The next day, Ed was due to go for his MRI; it was a busy week in the hospital with his other appointment booked for the following day. Sandi had taken time off to be with him on both appointments. They were sitting there talking about going down to Surrey the next weekend, and they had booked their travel arrangements. They had decided to fly down. It was also pointed out to him by Sandi that the train would have meant six hours without a cigarette. He had said that wouldn't have been a problem: he would have bought an e-cigarette. But Ed was glad that he was flying. It did mean he would be there more quickly and there would only be three hours without smoking.

As their food was placed in front of them, Weegie showed up. He was wearing the coat that Ed had bought him for the funeral, and it appeared well looked after.

"Hello to you two," he said, sitting in one of the spare seats beside them.

"I am intrigued that his daughters were the image of Catherine. Is he related to her in some way?" Jack asked.

"Hi, Weegie. How are you now?" Sandi asked. "Do you want to eat?"

"No, I am good," he replied and went on to say that Kenny had been down to see him and that he wanted to help out. "So we are opening a shelter of our own. I am going to live there, and it is going to help the homeless and vulnerable people out there. It was something that Fiona had been trying to set up, just before her death."

Weegie went on to say that part of the will had set aside a significant portion of her wealth to run the project. The children had got together and decided the best person to run it was their father. He pulled out a smartphone. "I don't know how it works, but it's nice to hear my children on the end of it."

Both Ed and Sandi commented on how he had changed. "Ask him!" Jack shouted within Ed's head.

"No," Ed answered him within his head. "I will not be party to your games."

Weegie went into how the charity would be set up. That in the past, poverty had been viewed as a lack of material things or maybe money. However, with the changes in benefits and the influx of immigrants, poverty and the effects it had on people were becoming much more complicated.

"Ask him!" Jack shouted.

There had always been links between impoverishment and poor health or unemployment, and this charity would be seeking to relieve and possibly prevent poverty. This would

CHAPTER 24

mean that Kenny would be carrying on his mother's work and would be working hard with health authorities to keep people with any health issues housed.

"Ask him!!" Jack bellowed.

On top of this, Weegie would be working a new shelter they were opening in the city, and this one was there for those that had already fallen through the cracks. It was going to have advisers coming in to help with housing issues and possibly getting people housed. Then, once safe, keeping them safe. They would also assist them with benefit claims and potential employment.

The family were all excited that they could do something to reach out to their missing father, but also keep their mother's dream alive. There was talk about buying property and converting it into bedsits for the people who needed them, actually giving them affordable housing.

"NOW, I WANT THE ANSWER!" Jack shouted.

Sandi commented on how good it all seemed but was worried that Weegie would struggle in a lovely cosy flat. "Oh, I am not leaving the streets. I have been on them nigh on thirty years. I had enough trouble sleeping on your bed. But I will be more in touch with the kids, and they need th …"

"Wee … NO," Ed suddenly shouted and stood up, knocking the chair flying behind him. Ed felt like his head was going to explode as Jack roared demands in his skull. Both Sandi and Weegie looked up at him, as did the couple walking past the pub.

"Are you okay?" Weegie asked.

"Yes, sorry." Ed looked at Sandi. "I need to go home, NOW." He moved to get out from behind the table and, as he did, his legs gave way, causing him to fall to the floor.

25

I am awake in London and stand there in the dark, damp and cold street of the year 1888. I am stunned because the last I remember is listening to Weegie and Sandi talking about the new charity. I had Jack asking me to ask Weegie something, but what I don't know. All I remember is telling him to go and then being here.

I ask Jack the date and time, and he informs me that it is 8th November and the night is early, just before seven o'clock.

There is a drizzle coming down and, as we stand on this corner, I feel it get heavier. I look around to see where I am exactly and see that I am on Miller Court. Jack seems to be watching the building across the way and, much as I would like to look about, he is insisting on just standing there.

I know why we are here and I know I can't stop it. The rain is getting heavier, and Jack steps back further into the doorway, hoping to keep dry.

Suddenly there is movement, and a young lady comes out of the now open door. She is shouting something back into the room behind her. She closes the door and walks to another door and goes in.

I want to get away from this scene that I have read all about. I know what is going to happen. I want to go back to the streets of Glasgow and be drinking beer with Sandi and Weegie, toasting

CHAPTER 25

his new life.

I can remember sitting there listening to the two of them talk. I had been petrified to say anything. I had this madman in my head demanding that I question Weegie about his daughters. Jack had tried to control me and my emotions. He was telling me that he was finished in London and now he needed my help to carry on his murderous way in Scotland.

He was telling me how he could direct me. Jack would suggest the best weapon for me to use in the killings, the perfect knives that would make the best cuts. He had watched me as I had used the keyboard and vision maker and he was sure that would help ensure they succeeded in 2016.

I got so frightened listening to him and his crazy thoughts that I would kill for him. "No, Mr Edward, I will kill, you will just be my vessel. You have no stomach for it." Jack had carried on for a while, and it was only when he had tried to speak to me that I lost it. It was the afternoon when I was sitting there with Sandi and Weegie. Weegie was telling us about how things were going with his children when my mouth opened and Jack started to talk.

I remember the moment Jack began to form words for me. "Weegie, do you know the name Eddowes?" was repeated over and over again, until I felt myself starting to say Weegie's name.

"Yes, Mr Edward, you disappointed me. I had such plans. Now I am stuck here until you awaken. Then we can plan the murder of deserving women in your time," Jack said. "So, until then, I am going to have fun here."

As we were standing there, the door opened again, and a man stepped out. "Barnett," Jack said. "Will he never learn? The girl is a whore and nothing more. I don't understand why he keeps coming back. Well, after tonight …"

Jack's laugh was deep. "This is going to be a long night, Mr Edward." I sigh – knowing this madman as I feel I do, I know he is right. I want so much at the moment to be away from here and talking to Sandi, getting things ready for Christmas. It is going to be an excellent holiday. My mother is not as bad as I make her out to be. I know if I can show her that Sandi is my life now and, if I finish this book, I can stay in Glasgow with Sandi and I know she is going to say yes to marrying me.

But I need to get out of this hellhole now. I don't want to see the murder and mutilation of Mary Jane Kelly. I saw the grainy photos of her body when it will be found tomorrow morning. I don't want to wake up knowing I had been part of it. I was having problems dealing with seeing the knives being used on other women, as well as the attack on Emma.

As I am trying to "will" myself awake, I watch the door open, and a strikingly blonde, young girl, and she is just a girl, walks out. She is tall. That is evident from her stance. She is standing tall and almost with an air about her. She is dressed in black, a black robe over a black dress and a black bonnet, which everyone seemed to adorn. I do wonder whether it is out of respect for the Queen and her extended period of mourning, or just that black hides more dirt?

I know instantly this is Mary and Jack leaves the shelter of the doorway to follow her. We walk behind her as she makes her way up to Commercial Road, ducking into doorways and alleys as she occasionally turns to see if she is being followed.

We reach the main road, and she stands there for a moment looking at the people milling about. From across the cobbles, there is a shout of "Mary", and Mary lifts her arm and waves to a woman standing at the entrance of the Ten Bells public house. With care, but also confidence, Mary crosses the street, avoiding the large shire horse left to die there. The two embrace and walk into the pub. We follow.

As we step inside, we see the two women moving to sit down on the stools in what I would call a snug. Jack orders a tankard from the same woman that had served us all those weeks ago. She still has no teeth and this time there is a lit pipe hanging out of her mouth, which she puffed on as she pulled the beer.

We take a seat by the window and can see the two women just over to the left of where we are sitting. They seem to be deep in conversation, with the occasional giggle and outright laugh. It was the same way I have seen girls talk when out in my time. That hasn't changed. I just wondered how the conversations varied.

I still can't get used to this smell and the taste of the beer. "Yes, Mr Edward, your time is better. I feel at home there, and I am sure we will have some adventures." As he is talking, the other woman gets up and goes to the bar and says something to the barmaid, who strikes a match on a brick on the bar and uses it as she puffs on the pipe.

After ensuring the tobacco is lit, she pulls out two shot glasses from below the counter and goes to a barrel at the end of the bar.

"Ah. We are on the gin tonight," says Jack. "Have you tried it, Mr Edward?" We are standing and moving to the bar. "Gin, please, wench." he demands and throws a coin at the woman when she brings back the glass. As Jack lifts it to his lips, I notice that the glass is smudged and there is what I assume to be a fly in it. But Jack gulps it down in one go. The taste is no different to what I know, but I worry about the fly.

26

I am finding that I have plenty of time this night to ponder things that have happened over the past few weeks. Somehow I had woken in this man's head, and I was experiencing his madness. His need to control and take life. I know that he is deep in my psyche now and, to be honest, much as I want to go back to my city and Sandi and that life, I am now petrified that if I wake up, I will not lose Jack. His presence is now so intense that I feel I will not be me anymore. I will all be Jack.

"No, Mr Edward. I will need you for a short time. I will need you to show me how to live in your day. I am a fast learner, so your part in this will only be short." We are sat in the Britannia having followed the two women out of the Ten Bells to here.

The two are getting very drunk, and it is only 10.30 p.m. That said, I have been in this time for nearly four hours and that is the longest I think I have ever been with Jack in his city. In my town, it was almost continuous. That is how I see it; I can't talk about times anymore. I live in a previous era. I can smell these streets and people. I just can't communicate.

I can feel this man's power and confidence growing as we sit there. He calmly watches Mary as she says goodbye to her friend at the door. I wonder how that goodbye would be if these two knew they were never going to see each other again.

There is a stab in my heart as I suddenly realise that if I do

CHAPTER 26

wake up, then I can never see Sandi again. And I can never tell her why. Jack, I know, will not allow that. Just as I know that if I tried to let the police know the truth, I would not be believed. I don't buy it, and I am living this nightmare.

What would happen if I did do that? If I managed to tell someone that I am Jack the Ripper? I know I would be ridiculed. It would be classed as a publicity stunt for my book. My book. would I be able to finish it? No, but that wouldn't stop people speculating that this was the reason it never got finished.

"Mr Edward, I want nothing to change in your life. I want you to carry on living your life the way you do. But there will be rules and the authorities are one of them. I like the thought of stability and a lover in the bed so Miss Sandi will stay, although it will be me with her night after night after you have instructed me on your ways." He laughed. "I hope I can be as intense with her as you are. However, in time she will grow to enjoy the new tricks I am to show her, I am sure."

I found myself gagging at this and was finding it hard to hold down the vomit I felt inside me trying to escape. I suddenly realised we were outside in a doorway and because I could no longer keep it down, I threw up into the gutter.

"Better?" he asked as he used the back of his hand to wipe his mouth. "You will grow accustomed to this new life, as I am with yours." Stepping over the vomit in the street, we followed Mary. Then, just as suddenly, she stopped and smiled at someone coming towards her. They were stood under the street lamp for a moment talking quietly to each other.

He was very young, about her age, and from what I could see exquisite looking with a blonde moustache and very well dressed, in a black morning suit and top hat. He took her by the arm and turned Mary towards and back into the pub. We moved back into the shadows and stood there. Jack seemed to act as if he was waiting for someone, turning this way and that, as people came down the street.

I notice a strange woman stood on the corner where Mary had just been and just for a moment I think it is Sandi. I try to call out to her, but she moves away as if being guided away from me. The weird thing about this woman is that she is dressed as I had last seen Sandi. She is wearing her cream wool coat, but it is undone and, considering the temperature, doesn't seem right. Also, she is holding her hat and gloves in her hands.

She is crying, too, and as I lose sight of her, I see her raise her hands with the hat and gloves to her nose. I find myself praying it is just a vision, and Jack hasn't seen her. And just as I felt I had seen Sandi, there too was Weegie, walking in the same direction that she had just gone. I am suddenly sick again and Jack, I sense, is not amused.

"Mr Edward, this must stop. You must learn to control this function," he chides me. We turn back towards the pub. After Jack has wiped his mouth again, we watch Mary exit.

She is stumbling as she walks, no longer the tall, confident girl, now Mary is walking slowly and having to think about every step as she avoids the sick we left on the path, making her way back towards her lodgings.

27

"Hi. How are you feeling?" It was the first time Ed had heard Sandi's voice in what seemed a lifetime, and it was the sweetest sound he had ever heard.

"Good, I think. Got a stonking headache, though." He tried to smile, but the effort was too much. He turned his head to the left, even though the actual action made him feel woozy, but he wanted to understand what the beeping sound was.

As his eyes were adjusting to the room again, he saw his mum sitting there with his dad standing behind her. She gave him a tearful smile and reached out her hand to touch his cheek.

"Okay, guys, we need to give Ed space and he will need to rest, so visiting is over for today." His mum's eyes looked up at where the male voice had come from and just for a second she seemed about to say something angrily, but Ed caught his dad raise his hand to her shoulder and gently squeeze it. His mum calmed and lowered her eyes back to Ed and stood towards him.

"I love you, Edward, and don't forget it," she said as she kissed him on the cheek.

She stood and made way for his father, who bent forward too and kissed his cheek. "Don't scare your mother like that again." Ed started to shake his head but stopped when nausea caught him in the chest. "See you tomorrow, son." He moved away and taking his mum by the arm, they left his line of vision.

"Ed?" He turned his head slowly to be met by Sandi's eyes. "Hi. I have got to go. We are staying at your place, so we will all be here tomorrow." She leant forward and kissed him on his lips for a few moments before the male voice sounded again.

"He will still be here tomorrow," was all Ed heard and was cross with it for taking Sandi away. But as she got up and disappeared as his parents had done, a man in a white tunic came into view with a cup of ice cubes in his hand.

Ed forgot his family and Sandi at the sight of this cup. He hadn't realised how parched he felt until that moment.

As the ice cubes were removed and handed to Ed with the gloved hand of the nurse, he said: "Well, you gave everybody a bit of a turn, but we have you now, and it will get better." The nurse smiled, and as Ed took the cube and as the water melted in his hands, Ed moved his hand to his mouth and sucked on it hungrily.

"Wow, there, don't overdo it, or you'll be sick again. By the way, my name is Josh, and I am the nurse assigned to look after you." His voice was soft and reassuring to Ed. Although he had to admit, he had no idea what was going on and had to ask Josh, just as soon as the cold water hit the back of his throat.

Josh then explained that four days ago, he and Sandi and Weegie had been sitting in a bar in the city and Ed had become very aggressive, to the extent that the police had been called. Ed tried to remember this, but his memory was blank. So, Josh continued. Ed had been shocked to hear that it had been that long ago. To him, it had only been eight hours.

"Oh, don't worry, you weren't violent towards Sandi or Weegie. The person you were angry with was you. You were shouting about something being in your head and wanting it out. Then you collapsed, and the police called for an ambulance,"

CHAPTER 27

Josh explained. "Well, the paramedics brought you here. Your blood pressure was through the roof, and your pulse was racing. So, you needed medical attention."

He went on to explain that when Ed was admitted into A&E, the first thing that the staff did was check his blood. "But it was your Sandi who told them about your visions, so we carried out an MRI and found the thing." Josh smiled at him. "And you are one lucky man."

The doctors had found a malignant tumour in his olfactory nerve area. They were waiting for pathology to confirm what type it was, then they could start the correct chemotherapy and radiation. Cancer in this area is rare, and one possibility was olfactory neuroblastoma, but the other types were undifferentiated carcinoma or lymphoma.

All Josh would say on the prognosis was that Ed's luck had been in. The hospital had a visiting professor over from the John Hopkins Hospital in the USA who had just completed a paper on cancer in this area of the brain recently and had offered to take the case on as Ed's consultant.

"Bit of a feather in his cap, he can use you and your treatment for another paper." Josh rolled his eyes and smiled. "And people ask me why I am not a doctor?"

It wasn't the hallucinations that had pointed them in this direction, but the fact that Sandi had said that over the past month Ed had been complaining about the horrible smells and this may have triggered a memory that had started the visions.

"When you are better, you can think about that and talk to the doctors," Josh carried on saying. "But you do know you will be in here over Christmas and Hogmanay. You have a long way to go." He handed Ed another ice cube and smiled.

Josh carried on explaining that, after the MRI had shown this vast mass, they had decided to operate and to remove as much of the affected tissue as they could and then use chemo and radiation to shrink the remaining tumour.

"I will be honest, and I think you need to know this now, this is going to be a long, long process and it may not work, but you have to give it a go, okay?" Ed nodded his head. He was tired now. He had a lot to think about, but first he needed sleep and, as if Josh could read his mind, he told him that he would be back soon to take his vitals. "But close your eyes for now."

As Ed shut his eyes to sleep, a tear rolled down his face.

28

"Do you want to hear this?" Ed said, looking into Sandi's eyes. He was sat up for the first time in days and was feeling a lot better than he had in a while.

It had been a hard few days, but tomorrow was Christmas Day and the family, who had rushed up to see him, were coming in for the party the neurology ward had organised. It was going to be a bit low-key to what Ed and his family were used to, but at least they were together.

Shortly after the New Year, there were plans to move Ed to the oncology department where he would start his chemotherapy and radiation treatment. This was going to be an initial four-week, high-dose course, with the hope that the majority of the tumour had shrunk. If that were the case, Ed would be able to go home and carry on the treatment as an outpatient for the remaining doses needed.

The family and Ed had asked whether, as Ed had recovered so well from the surgery, he could go home for the holidays. His specialist Dr Sampson said that because of the severity of the illness and the fact that he had collapsed and been in an induced coma for so long, it wasn't wise.

"Yes, I am dying to hear the end of the story," Sandi answered, taking hold of his hand. She was happy to see some colour had returned to his face. It had scared her so much when he had collapsed. It wasn't the screaming and shouting before. That wasn't frightening. She had known that he had had problems with the illusion of Jack being with him all the time after the funeral.

He had told her that the vision and voice were there all the time he was awake and the only time he could get away from Jack was when he slept. That was why his sleep patterns had changed, why he was tired so much.

While he had been in here, she had reread his book and spoken to Sam in Edinburgh about it. Sam had said that the story was good, but needed a dramatic ending. If Ed were going to expose the name of the Ripper, he would have to have concrete evidence to back it up. That was the problem with this type of story: people were all experts on the subject.

In Sam's opinion, the story wouldn't work without that. And to get the right ending, it would take years to research, to check every bit of evidence there was. When Sam had learnt about Ed's tumour, he had told Sandi that they should drop the book idea and concentrate on recovery. Sandi had thanked him and had just told Ed about the conversation.

Ed had been upbeat and said that, because he had been lying here, he had been trying to put his health in perspective and to come to terms with how his life would be for the next few years. He knew that this illness was not short term. It was up to three months of treatment and then extended physiotherapy for about a year.

But that wasn't the end – he would then have to have regular check-ups for years until they were sure the tumour had shrunk enough. But as Dr Sampson had said, that was if the treatment worked ...

But he was not going to think about that. He had to be

CHAPTER 28

positive. Tomorrow, Ed was going to tell his parents that he and Sandi were getting married. Sandi had said to him a few days ago that she would marry him. She had hoped to tell him on Christmas Day, but the fear of losing him had made her answer him now.

"Okay, he ..." Ed started to say as the door opened and in walked Weegie with a bottle of Lucozade and a big basket of fruit. "Wow. That's a lot of fruit, Weegie. Is it all for me? And why Lucozade?"

"Aye, sorry, ah didn't ken whit tae git, sae ah juist tellt th' lassie tae pat in a' th' fruit she hud. 'ere ..." He held his arms out to give it to Ed. Sandi stood up and took it from him to place on the unit by Ed's bed. "Whin ah wis a bairn mah ma aye gave me Lucozade. She said 'twas th' best dram tae mak' ye better."

Ed looked at him for a moment, before laughing. "Well, let's hope she was right. Take a seat, I was just going to tell Sandi about my last vision."

Weegie moved, a bit awkwardly, to the extra chair at the other side of the bed. "Urr ye aff tae be okay?" he asked. Weegie hated hospitals. He had not been in one for nearly thirty years, and that had almost killed him, but here was a young man that he had grown fond of who was going to be fighting for his life and it worried him.

"Honest answer, I don't know. But I am not giving up. There is so much research into all cancers, and I do have a fighting chance. But hey, let's not think about that today. Do you want to hear this or what?"

29

God, why am I still here? When am I going to wake up? We have been following Mary all night. I know it must nearly be 2 a.m., I asked, and Jack uttered that it was 1.50 a.m. a little while ago. Again, we are still hidden in the doorways, moving along if someone walks towards us.

Jack is not impressed with me. I know that his mood has turned very dark and he is not answering me when I try to talk to him. I couldn't help the sickness, but I am glad that it seems to have eased now. Although I had to ask, what was that noise? Jack was oblivious to it, and although I could clearly hear a mechanical sound all around me, he was getting angrier with me as I commented on it.

Mary's singing had helped to drown it out a bit. But that has stopped now, and the street is eerily quiet.

When we arrived back at Miller's Court, Mary and a man she had met as he was buying a "pail of ale" from a vendor on Commercial Street were stood outside her rooms and drinking the beer. Like so many of the men here, he is shabbily dressed in a long overcoat and wearing a billycock hat. His face is blotchy with small side whiskers and a carrot-coloured moustache.

One of the other prostitutes that lived on the street with Mary returned home. She looked cold and had her robe wrapped tightly around her. As the woman passes Mary, the man shouts out a very incoherent "Goodnight". To which Mary replies, "Goodnight. I am going to sing to you." Then within minutes, Mary was singing:

CHAPTER 29

"But while life does remain in memoriam, I'll retain, this small violet

I pluck'd from mother's grave.

Only a violet I pluck'd when but a boy, And oft'times when I'm sad at heart this Flower has giv'n me joy; so while life Does remain in memoriam I'll retain,

This small violet I pluck'd from mother's grave."

The two of them are alone now, and the song was repeated over and over by Mary as they drank. After a while, he left and she went into her rooms. Within minutes, the other lady had come back out again and walked towards Commercial Street.

Then we watched the man come back with a newspaper package, and he knocked three times on the window. She opened it full and with a quick kiss and a few words took it from him. Then he was gone.

The noise I thought I was imagining stopped a while ago, but now I have the sensation of something hammering, not loudly, just a gentle tapping. It was a shame Mary had stopped singing. Although it was only a few moments ago, I wonder how many unhappy people there must be in the road, trying to sleep. I had seen a couple of lights flicker from some of the windows around hers. She had been loud.

Even when the other lady had returned home again, Mary was still singing, and there was light coming from her room. It was only a short stay. The woman went through the door, came back out a minute or two later and travelled back to Commercial Road.

We watched another lady standing at the entrance to Miller's Court waiting for someone, close to Mary's window, for about half an hour, and then she went into one of the rooms and then out into another. I thought she entered the room the returning prostitute had gone into, but the hammering I could hear was distracting me. The singing had finished by then, and the Court seemed to be quietening down.

was at this point that Mary left to take a walk and she passed a man on Commercial Street and spoke to him. "Mr Hutchinson, can you lend me sixpence?"

"I can't," he answered, "I spent all my money going down to Romford."

"Good morning to you," Mary replied. "I must go and find some money." *She then walked towards Thrawl Street.*

Then Jack approached her and laid both his hands on Mary's shoulder. "Beautiful voice, my girl. I will give a sixpence to hear it again." *They both laughed. I have no idea why that was funny. She is even more pretty up close. Her skin is pale, and her hair untidily tucked inside her bonnet.*

"All right," Mary replied.

"You will be good for what I have told you," Jack responded, *then put his right hand on Mary's shoulder, and we began walking back towards Dorset Street.*

"All right, my dear. Come along. You will be comfortable." *And he put his arm around Mary, and she let up and kissed him.*

"I've lost my handkerchief," she said. *To this Jack pulled out a red handkerchief and handed it to her.*

We have reached her rooms by now, and she opens the door to let us in. The room is small, and there is a small table under the window with the remains of a fish dinner in the newspaper sat upon it. There is a single bed pushed into the other corner furthest from the door, and the sheets are unmade and creased.

There is a strong smell of burning that is getting stronger, and we stand there.

Suddenly I hear her say something. I can't make it out, but Jack is frenzied as he pushes Mary onto the bed. He takes the package that I just noticed was in his hand and places it on the table. Mary moves to get up, but he strikes out at her, hitting her across the face.

CHAPTER 29

She stumbles back and hits the wall before collapsing on the bed. For a moment, I think she has died, but then I hear her mumble the words.

"Help me, please. Someone, save me."

There is a throaty laugh from Jack as he pulls out a knife. The smell of burning is getting stronger, and I realise that Jack is staring at me, with a questioning look on his face. I am standing behind him, and he is shouting, "I will murder. It is my right to murder. YOU. WILL. NOT. STOP. ME." And he turns back to Mary.

I am trying to move forward to stop him from harming her. I grab for his arm, but my arms can't move. I try to shout, but my voice box is paralysed. I am powerless. All I can do is watch this madman hack at the poor girl on the bed.

As the brutality of the crime unfolds, I fear that he is still there, telling me that I am not rid of him, that our work together will not end tonight. But as he mutilates Mary, I can feel him getting weaker and weaker until suddenly he is gone and I am looking at the body of what was a vibrant woman, and I start to cry.

I have just witnessed a stranger mutilate many women over the past month or so, but this time was different. I stood behind him; I had watched him use the knife on Mary, I had watched the blood spray against the wall as she died.

But the worst was that I had seen the face of Jack. He had turned and looked at me, and that was the most horrific sight. The face that had looked back at me at that moment was my own. It was me that screamed and cursed. It was me that had taken up that knife and destroyed all these lives. But why?

I don't know how long I stood there, alone, scared of what I was becoming or rather what I had become. I was a killer, a murderer from the 19th century and I needed to be stopped. But how?

Suddenly, while I was trying to figure out how to stop this, I heard

JACK

someone say my name, over and over again. There was a hand resting on my shoulder, and I could smell disinfectant and cleanliness.

A nurse is smiling at me telling me it's gone, and I am okay, now. The doctors got it all.

Jack had gone.

BIBLIOGRAPHY

This is just a selection of where I went to research this story. I know there are probably more sites I looked at so I would like to thank you all for being there ...

www.jack-the-ripper-tour.com

http://www.casebook.org

https://en.wikipedia.org/wiki/Jack_the_Ripper

http://www.victorianweb.org/history/slums.html

http://www.jtrforums.com/index.php

http://www.historyhouse.co.uk/articles/jack_the_ripper.html

http://victorianripper.niceboard.org/

Cover copyright via;
  www.123rf.com/profile_neillang

Now all the slushy bit ...
A big thank you goes out to all the wonderful sites there are

on the web on Jack the Ripper that helped me write this.

Now I have got to thank the people who made this happen. Adam, my husband, who has put up with me obsessing over the subject. My mum, Elspeth Jones, for being my biggest critic.

Mark Desmond Hughes for spending a weekend proofing it. Theo for pushing me to finish it. And Mark Swift, for giving it that polished touch.

I hope you enjoyed it. And I know I could write more, but do you really read it?

Email at sheenah.middle@gmail.com if you do!

One last thing ... Please review the book, as that will help with future sales.

Made in the USA
Middletown, DE
21 July 2018